BILLIONAIRE IN DISGUISE

MELANIE KNIGHT

WINDYHOPE STAR PRESS

To my Aunt Adrienne
Thank you for a thousand beautiful memories, a million smiles and never-ending love.
You are forever in my heart.

ABOUT BILLIONAIRE IN DISGUISE

Wanted: Fake boyfriend

Qualifications: Must be charming and friendly. No criminal masterminds. Prior experience as a fake boyfriend a plus.

Responsibilities: Convince my large family you are my boyfriend, so I don't ruin their celebration. May involve shirtless jogs, splash fights and lots of practice kissing.

Applicant Name: Dominick Knight, a.k.a. Nick Walters

Employment: Billionaire CEO of Knight Technology, undercover as a temp to investigate corruption.

Special skills: Keeping my true identity a secret.

Final result: Secrets, seduction and excitement.

CHAPTER 1

"Who are you?"
"I am not as I appear."
"That is obvious."

He was an idiosyncrasy, an anomaly in a plush perfect world of garish luxury. Floor-to-ceiling windows streamed light to a wall of mirrors, illuminating the stark white angles of ultra-modern furniture and a massive blood red desk. Million-dollar statues rose like crystal daggers, their jagged edges reflecting the eerie translucent visage of a stranger's face. No one would recognize Dominick Knight, billionaire businessman, computer genius and international bestselling author, next to the garish marble furnishings of the gleaming penthouse.

That was the point.

Of course, not everything was different. His eyes still glinted like blue diamond shards; his hair remained a whisper past midnight. He stood the same formidable height, his muscular build a testament to the hours he spent at the gym. Yet beyond that the changes were stark:

A once clean-shaven face hidden behind a dark beard.

Baggy, ill-fitting clothing, two decades out of season, plucked from a discount chain's clearance rack.

Thick glasses reminiscent of his grandfather's time.

"Who do you think I am?"

The thin, balding man encircled him, his thousand-dollar Armani pebbled leather shoes echoing on the polished ceramic floor. His confusion was expected, assured even. "A billionaire risking everything with a game. What will the media say when they discover the truth?"

They would never leave him alone.

Yet it didn't matter. Dominick stepped forward, tracing his hand along the priceless grand piano no one played. "Are they happy?"

"Who?" Montgomery Carlyle lifted a hand adorned with thick diamond rings. His voice was nasal, from a nose that grew thinner with every visit to his famed plastic surgeon.

Dominick set his jaw. He had already explained the plan twice. "My employees."

"Your employees?" The answer was as chilled as the temperature. "Does it matter?"

Dominick tightened, stepped to the crystal-clear panes showcasing the brilliant Miami skyline. The buildings soared all around them, scraping the sky with their gilded architecture. Few rose as high as his penthouse office. "The rumors portray problems far beyond a difficult work environment. I must see for myself." Many in his position wouldn't care, secure at the crescendo of society.

That wasn't who he was.

Carlyle lifted a bony shoulder. "Even with your disguise, the risk of discovery is significant. Your face has graced the cover of every society page on the Internet, and that was before your bestselling book was crowned motivational book of the year. Whether you like it or not, you are a celebrity. What will you do if they uncover your identity?"

The already intense media scrutiny would increase a thousandfold. Life would never be the same. "The risk is irrelevant. To them, I will just be an ordinary employee."

"There is nothing ordinary about you."

Dominick stood tall, folded his arms across his chest. "No one will discover the truth."

"I hope so," Carlyle replied. "Because if you're not careful, you'll end up on every news station across the country."

Yes, he would.

※

"Bring your boyfriend." The words glared from Adrianna Lewis' small cell phone screen.

Three words.

One sentence.

Inescapable consequences.

"What did you say?"

Adrianna gasped and pivoted, relaxed only slightly as the speaker pushed herself off the neon yellow wall. She sucked in a breath of orange-scented air, management's newest ~~torture~~ work-improving technique, and cringed at the bitter taste. "Don't do that, Chloe. I thought you were Mr. Dobbs."

Chloe merely shook her head before sitting on one of the round rolling stools. Too fast, as she rolled forward, and then to the side, then back again. With a whoosh, the stool went down, and then up, bobbing her blond curls like a slinky. "Why can't we get normal chairs like everyone else?"

"Because these keep you alert and effective, ready to build the technology that changes the world." With a deep voice, Adrianna rattled off the Knight Technology memo, which arrived the day her sturdy chair had been replaced with a tiny stool that didn't cover half her–

"Ass."

"What?"

"Dobbs is an ass. Why do you care if he sees you on your cell phone? You deserve your twenty-seven minute lunch."

"Haven't you heard? Our lunch allotment has decreased to twenty-six minutes. For our benefit, of course."

Benefits noted thus far:

1. A delightful tangle of hunger pains and indigestion

2. Increased budget for antacids

3. Running to the ladies' room had become a spectator sport.

"I can't afford to lose this job, at least not yet."

"You know my opinion." Chloe patted down her smart aqua pantsuit and lowered her voice. "I have an interview today."

Adrianna smoothed her own floral dress. Everyone was searching for a way to escape Dobbs' Dungeon, the Ft. Lauderdale office of Knight Technology and remnant of her dream job. It had started so well, with fantastic pay, excellent work conditions and the chance to join the cutting-edge leader of the industry. Then Dobbs arrived, and everything changed.

Chairs shrunk. Lunch hours shrunk. Management complaints skyrocketed. Yet still she endured. She didn't want a job at any company. As soon as she saved up enough, she'd *build* one.

"Back to earlier." Chloe peered at Adrianna's cell phone. "I must have misheard. I thought you said—"

"Read it." Adrianna held out the offending device. "When you finish, you can help me find an island where I can hide for the next six months."

Chloe took the smartphone with one red-manicured hand. Her eyes darted back and forth, eyebrows rising almost as high as the purple polka-dotted umbrellas hanging off the ceiling. "You have a boyfriend? Where did you hide him? Are you getting married? Can I be your maid of honor?"

"No, in my imagination and only if you want an invisible groom." Adrianna took the phone back and dumped it in her purse. "I don't have a boyfriend."

Chloe folded her arms across her chest. "Explain."

"The e-mail is from my mother. I may have inadvertently given her the idea I had a boyfriend."

"How did you inadvertently do that?"

"I told her I have a boyfriend." Adrianna grimaced. "Now she wants to meet my boyfriend, and she would be disappointed to learn he's existence challenged." She thumped her fingers against the particle board desk. "I can't believe how many times she's asked about him."

Chloe blinked. "Your mother still makes you eat four and a half vegetables a day. Why wouldn't she ask about a boyfriend?"

"Just because she says something doesn't mean I listen." Adrianna discreetly pushed aside her spinach, broccoli, carrot, asparagus and half a tomato sandwich. "In a few days, I was going to tell her we broke up."

"A few days." Chloe exhaled slowly. "I've had a dozen boyfriends that lasted that long. Just tell her you didn't like him after the second date and–"

"Six months."

Chloe stopped. "What?"

"It's been six months." *Give or take three.* "I said it as a joke, but she sounded so happy, I didn't have the heart to tell her the truth. I planned to eventually come clean, but I kept procrastinating. Now she's mentioned it to family, friends, work colleagues, the supermarket janitor, her dermatologist, the accountant and the mailman."

"Does the mailman's dog know?" Chloe asked dryly.

"Naturally." Adrianna picked the tomato off the sandwich. Technically a tomato was a fruit, so she hadn't truly followed her mother's dictates.

"So what changed?"

"Their anniversary." Throwing the *half-fruit* back, Adrianna stood. "When the office closes for renovations next week, I'm going to Orlando for the big celebration. My mother is insisting I bring Jonathon."

"You gave him a name?" Chloe stared.

"I couldn't tell my mother I didn't know his name, and Invisible Man seemed a little suspect." Adrianna held out her fingers. "I also gave him a job, hobbies, a favorite color…"

"Are you sure he doesn't exist?"

All too well. "She's asked about him visiting before. I always managed to avoid it, but this time she threatened to come here and introduce herself. It's been hard enough pretending he was away every time she's visited. I won't get away with it again."

"Why don't you just tell her you broke up?"

Adrianna braced her hands on the narrow desk. Apparently less work space meant more productivity, at least according to Mr. Dobbs. Still, she managed to fit a small picture of her parents on the one thin shelf. "Anniversaries are a big deal for my family. If we broke up, it would ruin the whole celebration."

"But you *will* break up afterwards."

"I promise." Adrianna held up her hand. "Although if I planned a pretend wedding, I wouldn't have to–"

"Adrianna!" Chloe hissed.

She smiled. "I'm joking. Right after their anniversary, this relationship is going to end." She frowned. "Or go back to not existing."

Chloe softened. "Why don't you let me introduce you to some guys? Half the men here are interested in you."

Adrianna opened her mouth to say no, yet hesitated. Perhaps it was time to consider other options. "When this is all over, you can tell me about some of them."

Chloe brightened. "Fantastic. Before I find you a real boyfriend, however, I'm going to find you a fake one."

"I'm sorry?" Adrianna blinked. "You do realize he can't be invisible."

"I considered it. But that would be a stretch, even for me." Chloe waved her hand. "How long is the trip?"

"An entire week." Seven days of pitying looks and enough comfort food to last a year.

Note to self: pack extra antacids.

"An entire week." Chloe whistled lowly, scanning the workers packed into their mini-desks and roly-poly stools. "It's lucky so many men work at computer companies."

"You're not suggesting I recruit someone from the office?" Adrianna gaped. "How would I face him afterwards? Plus, who would want to do that?"

"You'd be surprised." Chloe pivoted, yet her frown deepened with every man. "You're leaving the company, so who cares what they think? Plus, the office is closed all next week, so you know they'll have the time."

"I'm not quitting yet," Adrianna returned. "If my venture takes longer than expected, I don't want to run into my ex fake date by the water cooler."

"We don't have a water cooler anymore. Dobbs said it was superfluous, remember?" Chloe stopped, her lips curving into a slow, wide smile. "What about the new temp?"

"New temp?" Knight Technology didn't use temps. Whenever someone quit, the other employees just picked up the extra work. "I hadn't noticed him."

"Then you'd be the only one."

Adrianna followed her friend's pointed finger. Then she stopped...

And stared.

And stared some more.

And stared just a little more, simply because... wow.

The e-mail must have unbalanced her more than she realized to miss this man. Several inches above six feet, he was massive in a very, very, very (a hundred more verys) good way. His clothing was baggy, yet it couldn't hide broad shoulders, muscular arms or the backside that was as tight as– She cleared her throat. He had a beard, tousled hair and glasses he'd clearly stolen from someone's grandpa, yet despite it all, he was… "Gorgeous."

"Isn't he?" Chloe grinned. "It's like he's trying to hide behind those big glasses and that outfit. Yet somehow chic geek works for him. Actually a paper bag would work for him. Or better yet, nothing at–"

"Chloe!"

Her friend's smile only deepened. "All the ladies are eyeing him. He would definitely light up your celebration."

Yes, he would. "What should I do?" she mumbled. "Walk up to him and ask if he wants to be my fake boyfriend for the week?"

Chloe nodded. "Sounds like a plan."

"It's not a plan," Adrianna refuted. "He'll think I'm crazy."

"Probably."

"He'll laugh at me."

"That's a definite chance."

"He'll say no."

"Perhaps…" Chloe rubbed her hands together. "Or perhaps not. A free vacation is pretty attractive. He's new, so he probably wasn't expecting the time off. He might even consider it an adventure."

Adrianna peered closer. The man was adjusting and readjusting his seat, as if he couldn't quite discern how to fit on something so small. "He doesn't seem the sort who goes on adventures."

"Even better." Chloe gestured to the other employees. "He

doesn't know anyone here, so he's unlikely to gossip, and he'll be gone in a relatively short time. He's perfect."

Could she really do this? In the end, it was the outfit that convinced her.

No one who dressed like that could be anything other than he seemed.

※

THE OUTFIT HAD BEEN A MISTAKE.

It seemed like a good idea at the time. He certainly couldn't wear his five-thousand-dollar Armani suit, and he wanted to look as different as possible from Dominick Knight. So he found clothing two sizes too big and two decades too old, eschewed the products to style his hair and tried to blend into the background. In the end, he may not have been noticeable as the boss, but he was noticeable as *something*.

He squirmed in the rolling Frisbee that paraded as a chair. It felt like he was in a cheesy horror flick, complete with useless modern furnishings and fluorescent embellishments. His eyes hurt from staring at the neon walls, and his backside ached from a chair that didn't cover half his—

"Mr. Walters."

He looked into the beady eyes of the man who'd been introduced as his boss, Mr. Dobbs. He was not familiar with him, as hiring decisions at this level were well below CEO responsibility. He wore a designer suit, an expensive smartwatch and a consistent scowl. "I need you to clean the break room. There's a huge mess."

Dominick narrowed his eyes. The temp job was a relatively low one, yet it entailed only technical responsibilities. "Is that part of my position?" he asked carefully.

"Your position is whatever I tell you," Dobbs snapped. "If

you want to last more than an hour, get that kitchen clean. There's a rag under the sink."

The urge to reveal his true identity was almost more than he could resist, yet somehow he grumbled an affirmative as he lifted himself up. How could this be a Knight Technology office? Once, he'd managed every office, yet with thousands of employees spread across four continents, such attention had become impossible. Still, this never should've been allowed to happen.

Two men emerged from the break room as he approached. "I can't believe Dobbs was looking through my food again," one hissed. "What is wrong with the man?"

The other's expression was far more thunderous. "At least he didn't spill yours everywhere, then pretend it was his food. I wrote my name in three-inch letters."

So Dobbs rummaged through employees' food, spilled it and then asked someone else to clean it?

Yeah, he was so fired.

To call it a break room was as much a stretch as calling the rolling Frisbee a chair. It was the size of his college dorm room, or perhaps its attached closet, or perhaps the shoebox in the closet. It contained a half-size refrigerator, miniature microwave and several stools along a narrow counter. Oh, yes, and a plate of lasagna smeared across the floor.

It didn't make sense. Each Knight Technology office planned for a generous lounge with more than enough refrigeration, appliances and seating for all. Yet fresh drywall cut the room to a sliver, no doubt to the benefit of Dobbs' already large office on the other side. There was no need to guess where the complimentary assortment of snacks, coffees and pastries was located.

Was there a way to fire someone twice?

Dominick breathed deeply, choking as the overpowering odor of tomatoes and oregano coated his throat. He reached for the rag, stopped just before he touched the blackened scrap of filth. He grabbed the thin roll of paper towels instead, doubled them, and used the first to deposit the rag into the overfilling garbage. Then he used a dozen more to start cleaning the floor.

How many good employees had they lost because of Dobbs? How many more would they lose? Yet the rumored problems weren't limited to this office, with numerous Knight Technology locations reporting issues. Despite few official complaints, the rumors had gotten louder, amidst higher than expected turnover, especially considering the generous pay. Something was very, very wrong.

He tossed the red-soaked paper into the garbage, just as his telephone buzzed. He'd asked Carlyle not to call during work hours unless there was an emergency.

"Is everything all right?" Keeping his voice low, Dominick edged to the back of the room. Hopefully the lasagna explosion would keep others away.

"I'm sorry to bother you, but our newest software is showing some glitches. I have the CIO on the line."

"Of course." Dominick stayed silent as the executive outlined the problem. They traded various ideas, and, in a flurry of technical jargon, the problem was quickly resolved. "If you have any problems, let me know."

Carlyle returned to the phone. "There's one last thing. I want to confirm your satisfaction with the new cyber-security program. The final cost is nine point eight million."

"Under ten million dollars?" Dominick smiled. "That's a bargain. Go for it."

"Perfect. How are matters progressing there?"

Dominick took a step and almost slipped on a lasagna noodle. He grasped the counter to keep from falling. "It could be better."

For a moment, there was silence. "You found something?"

"Something disgusting." He threw the slimy remnants of a tomato into the garbage. "Literally. I will be making significant changes when I return. At least, the disguise worked perfectly. No one suspects who I really am."

A gasp sounded.

He froze. Swallowed. "I have to go."

Slowly, he pivoted. A woman stood watching him, as still and serious as midnight in the arctic winter. She was one of the mid-level software solutions technicians, a common position in the company, and yet she was anything but typical. He'd looked at her once when he arrived, then twice and three times. With a petite frame, generous curves and alluring features, she was lovely, and he'd had to stop himself from approaching her.

Now she stared at him, her deep black hair gleaming in the stark florescent lighting, her cat green eyes burning with intelligence and suspicion.

What had she heard? What had she realized? Most of all…

Did she know who he was?

CHAPTER 2

Who was he?

The question burned as stark as the spilled lasagna painting the counters, the floors and even the walls. Adrianna stepped into the tangy space, the sound of her no-nonsense pumps echoing on the dull grey tile, as she watched the man watching her.

For a moment, unease lit his eyes. It vanished an instant later, replaced by calm, cool control. This was a man who understood power.

He strode towards her, and she fought the urge to retreat. Perhaps she should leave now, make an excuse that the spilled food spoiled her appetite. Her stomach was unsettled, yet more from the man's stoic regard than any mess. On the phone, he'd admitted he was not as he seemed.

Who was he?

She should find someone else for her impossible plan. Only something compelled her to stay, even as the silence stretched. Perhaps he had a reasonable explanation for the cryptic words. "Are you a spy?"

She was only half-joking, yet his eyes widened. "Pardon me?"

Heat crept up her neck, and the reflection in the mirrored toaster showed a redness to rival the tomato sauce puddled on the floor. "You said no one suspects who you really are. That's something a spy would say."

He cocked his head to the side. "Do I look like a spy?"

The automatic negative caught in her throat. If one were going to pretend to be a spy, and not the three-piece suit variety like on a movie screen, then he may dress in the most unlikely way possible. An out-of-date and ill-fitting outfit?

Perhaps.

"If you aren't a spy, then perhaps a hero in disguise?"

A ghost of a smile appeared. "I'm afraid not."

"Please tell me you aren't a criminal."

He folded powerful arms. "Indeed I am. I contrived to steal the lasagna, only my plan went awry."

Her lips twitched. "I hadn't noticed."

He gestured to the lasagna coating every surface like a toddler's finger painting. "I am very subtle. After all, stealing lasagna is an art form."

She smiled. Her imagination had indeed gone awry. He was not a spy, criminal or secret hero, but just a man indulging in a private conversation, of which she had heard one side. "I'm sorry. I'm sure there's a good reason for what you said." Yet as she stood there, the silence resumed, and he said nothing.

Perhaps there was more to him than apparent.

Physically, he was even more impressive from up close. He stood a good three inches above six feet, a stark contrast to her frame of barely 5'2. Although he was tall, he was by no means lanky, with an expansive chest, solid arms and long legs. Chiseled features drew handsome lines, sensual lips and striking eyes.

"Do you think I have some deep, dark secret?" His deep murmur stole her attention, more as his stern visage melted into a lopsided grin. "I'm Nick Walters, the new temp. I'd shake your hand, but my palms are covered in mozzarella."

She cringed as he held up sauce-coated fingers. They were large and capable, just like the rest of him. "I'm Adrianna Lewis."

"Do all temps get such enjoyable work?"

She nodded, slanting him another look. Behind his glasses, his eyes were a deep blue, the color of the twilight sky. She forced her gaze back to the spilled food. "Actually, no one is safe from Dobbs' dirty work. I assume you didn't spill this?"

He shook his head. "It isn't even my food."

She looked upward, grabbed a handful of paper towels. She wiped a bell pepper off the counter. "I assume it wasn't Dobbs' food either, but he spilled it."

His gaze hardened. "Does this happen often?"

"With appalling regularity." She leaned down and wiped splatters of sauce off the drawers. "I would say he does it on purpose, but I've seen him. He's so preoccupied with pretending he isn't snooping, he gets clumsy."

"Why do I get the feeling this isn't his only unprofessional behavior?"

She opened her mouth, stopped and glanced towards the door. While she quietly shared her thoughts with Chloe, this man was a stranger. She needed this job, at least until she was ready to launch her own venture. "You're not a corporate spy, are you?"

For a moment, he hesitated, then he smiled again. "You figured it out. I'm in charge of the office. Actually, why stop there? I run the entire division."

She relaxed, pretending to swipe at him with the paper

towel. "Are you sure you don't own the company?" she teased.

"Of course, I do." His eyes lit with amusement. They really did sparkle–

Stop. She was here for a pretend date, not a real one. And if she wanted to solicit his help, she'd have to ask. Yet not here, and not now. Before she invited him into her life, if only temporarily, she needed to learn more about him. She couldn't do that with what remained of her rapidly dwindling lunch. "Would you like to go out with me?"

A slight narrowing of the eyes was the only sign of well-deserved incredulity. Of course, he was shocked. She'd asked him on a date after four and a half minutes. She should have waited at least ten. If she really wanted to take it slow, fifteen.

"Go out?" He lowered his gaze. "On a–"

"For dinner." A week of them, yet she would refrain from asking that until they had spoken for at least half an hour, as was only proper. She gripped the paper towel so hard it spritzed sauce back to the floor. She quickly swiped it up. "We could go after work, and I can tell you about the job. There's a great place across the street that has the most delicious lasagna and…" Her gaze snagged on his red hands. "They have sandwiches, too."

He blinked.

She tried to appear a little less deranged. "You seemed interested in the work environment."

A light entered his eyes, disappearing a second later. "I was just curious about the job."

"Of course." Obviously he was interested in learning about his new position, especially after the less-than-hospitable welcome from Dobbs. "Could it become permanent?"

"No." The response was immediate, succinct and final. It also brought unexpected dissatisfaction.

"All right."

"All right?"

His gaze was soft. "Why not?"

Why not indeed? "I'll meet you after work." She backed out slowly. "It's the restaurant with the big party hat out front. It's popular for people celebrating special occasions."

His expression softened. "That reminds me of my parents' anniversary next week. They're travelling now, but I want to prepare a little something for them when they return."

A sliver of tension melted. That their parents celebrated anniversaries on the same week could only be a sign.

Nick pulled out his phone and started typing. "I should make sure my assistant received the gift I ordered."

Her smile faltered. "Your assistant?"

He froze. After a silent moment, he cleared his throat and held up his cell. "I mean my phone. You know, one of those AI programs."

"Of course." Obviously, no temp had an assistant. Yet she didn't really know anything about him, except that he was a strange dresser and conducted mysterious conversations about who he really was.

And she was about to invite him to be her boyfriend.

Did she suspect the truth?

When Adrianna overheard his conversation, it seemed as if the investigation was over before it truly began. Mentioning his assistant was another unforced error, and she responded with clear suspicion. He selected personal gifts for his family and friends, but with his hectic schedule, an assistant was necessary. Hopefully, she'd accepted his explanation.

Since then, he'd caught her staring at him several times. The beard hid much of his famous face, yet it would not take much to discover the truth. Hopefully, she wouldn't contemplate the billionaire CEO of the company would masquerade as a temp.

He had done a little investigating into *her*. Her behavior had been just a tad too unusual, and he needed to ensure she wasn't a reporter who somehow uncovered his ruse. The personnel file had revealed an impressive resume, a magna cum laude degree from a highly-regarded school and exceptional performance reviews. References described her as easy-going, down to earth and completely normal.

Not the least bit like a woman who would ask a perfect stranger on a date.

She actually seemed pretty amazing, the sort of woman he would have asked on a real date. Yet he'd bet his brand new Ferrari she had an ulterior motive for inviting him to dinner. Perhaps she really did want to share office gossip, or she was looking to network in a bid to change positions. He couldn't blame her for wanting to escape.

Since he returned to his desk, Dobbs had instructed him to:

Run to the local coffee shop to fetch an extra-large, half-decaf, extra-whip, extra-caramel, light sugar and extra-milk coffee.

Water every plant in the office.

Clean up the mess when Dobbs spilled the extra-large, half-decaf, extra-whip, extra-caramel, light sugar and extra-milk coffee.

Unclog the toilet in the men's restroom.

Return to the coffee shop to replace the extra-large, half-decaf, extra-whip, extra-caramel, light sugar and extra-milk coffee.

He could fire him. Should fire him. Yet first he had to learn the extent of mismanagement, and how it was related to the other offices. Regional managers should have caught this. Why they hadn't was his first question.

For now he would observe, ask questions and discover what he could from Adrianna. He would have to be careful. Because if they discovered the truth, the world would descend.

"You made it."

"Did you think I wouldn't come?"

Most assuredly. "Not at all." Smiling widely, Adrianna gestured Nick inside the brightly lit space. "Ready?"

"After you." He held the door open, then followed her into the cozy pizzeria with red-checked tables, stained glass lamps and a miniature jukebox on each table. The aroma of fresh sauce and cheese wafted from a display of specialties, a heady accompaniment to the murmur of light conversation and laughter. It was welcoming and warm, a mom and pop with a quirky charm the chain stores could never quite emulate.

Adrianna chose a table in the corner, away from prying eyes. She murmured a thank you as Nick held out one of the vinyl-cushioned seats, as if they were on a real date. A pretty waitress handed them two menus, her eyes lingering on Nick just a tad longer than appropriate.

Adrianna frowned at the ridiculous urge to tell her to find her own fake boyfriend.

Nick smiled a lopsided grin that unsettled her stomach. She cleared her throat, straightened. This was the perfect opportunity to launch her speech, tell him why she'd really invited a perfect stranger to dinner. She'd be earnest and frank, explain her plan with logic and reason.

Instead, she picked up the large, laminated menu and buried her face in it.

Subtle.

She needed a few minutes to convince herself this was not completely crazy. Somewhat crazy, yes, mostly, perhaps. All right, completely crazy, yet she was determined. But first she was going to read the menu she already knew by heart, then read it again and again. And then again. After all, procrastination was an art form.

"Are you still deciding?" A disembodied voice came from beyond her makeshift shield, tinged with a dash of amusement and a heaping of confusion. She slammed the menu down, eliciting a startled look.

"Sorry." She half-chuckled, half-choked. The waitress returned with their waters, and Adrianna grasped her glass, gulping so much she *did* choke. Nick gazed at her in concern, handing her a napkin as she blinked away tears.

This was not going well.

The waitress didn't even look her way as she batted her eyelashes at Nick like a hummingbird's wings. "Do you know what you want? Today's special is lasagna."

Nick turned slightly green. "I think I'll stick with pizza." He paused. "Adrianna, do you want to split a pie?"

"Perfect." She wouldn't prolong this by a minute. She handed the menu to the waitress, and added one last fortification. "And some of your delicious garlic rolls."

The waitress gave Nick a saucy wink. "Coming right up."

Adrianna plastered a smile on her face. *Breathe.* She needed to stay calm, cool and collected to accomplish her goals. The first step: learning all about Nick Walters, subtlety of course. "Tell me everything about you."

Well, that was as subtle as a rhinoceros.

His eyes narrowed, and she just managed not to slink under the table. Now he probably thought she was unhinged *and* a stalker. "Actually don't tell me everything. Just the relevant parts."

Relevant parts:

1. Did he possess fake boyfriend experience?

2. What made him uniquely qualified for the position?

3. Did he take Fake Boyfriend 101 in college?

She should have typed up an application.

He traced the glass, as if trying to decide what to tell her. *Strange.* "There's not much to tell. I love the beach and warm weather and have always worked in computers. I needed an escape from my life and figured an internship would be perfect."

"Your life?" She tilted her head. "You're not really a criminal, are you?"

"I thought we'd already established I was."

"That's right." She smoothed her napkin. "You're the infamous lasagna thief. I should have brought you to a different restaurant."

"Too late now."

Some of the tension seeped out of her body. Perhaps *Fake Boyfriend 101* was unnecessary.

"I wanted to explore new places. Learn about different companies. So tell me–" He leaned forward. "Do you like working at Knight Technology?"

She brought the glass to her lips again, wetting her throat with the cool spring water. Should she be honest about the disaster the office had become? She glanced around, confirmed no other employees were present. "This stays between us." She lowered her voice. "I don't want to lose my job."

His eyes turned serious. "I promise this won't harm you in any way. Perhaps I could even help."

A temp had no power, yet it was kind of him to say. She hesitated, but only for a moment. He would soon learn what their work environment was like. "When I first started, Knight Technology was a fantastic place to be."

He smiled… until she added, "But it's become a nightmare." As his grin faded, she instinctively placed her hand over his. "Don't worry, it's not going to affect you, since you're a temp."

"I'm sorry it's affecting anyone."

"It isn't your fault."

By his hardened gaze, it didn't seem like he believed it. Yet he'd barely walked in the door of a company he would soon leave. He held no culpability. "Your boss is unbelievable. Does he drive people away?"

"Employees come and go with alarming frequency," she confirmed. "We lose a lot of good people, many of whom move on to make huge contributions to competitors. I've even gotten several offers." At his questioning expression, she shook her head. "I turned them down. I have other plans."

His face was a wall of granite. "Has anyone complained about Dobbs to higher management?"

"Again and again. It doesn't matter." She shook her head. "Word is he knows someone at the top. Anytime we say something, we're told it will be addressed, and nothing changes."

"That's going to change."

He said it with such certainty, it snagged her next words. Even if it was unlikely, he seemed to believe he could do something. She threaded her hands under her chin. "Do you know someone in upper management?"

He hesitated. "I could contact them."

"You'd be wasting your time," she warned, as she lifted her napkin off the table and placed it on her lap. "They don't care."

He visibly tightened, and suddenly he seemed a different man altogether. She peered closer. "If you don't mind my asking, how did you get the position? We've never had a temp before." His uncomfortable look returned, and the urge to make him feel better surged. "Let me guess. As a criminal boss, you snap your fingers, and people do whatever you want."

"That's right," he drawled. "I have thousands at my command."

"Do you?" She chuckled softly. "That must be fun."

"Actually it's exhausting." He almost sounded genuine. "What about you? You mentioned career plans."

She opened her mouth, just stopping herself from sharing her cybersecurity venture. Why did this man elicit her trust, even as he clearly hid his own secrets? "I'm working on several projects."

He unfolded his red-checked napkin. "As part of your position?"

"Not exactly."

He didn't have a chance to respond before the waitress returned with the pizza. Steam drifted from a hot pie with golden crust, hearty tomato sauce and mozzarella cheese melted to perfection. Nick served them each a thick slice and an oversized garlic roll drizzled with olive oil and roasted garlic.

She bit into her slice. The taste of fresh tomatoes, melt-in-your-mouth cheese and fresh herbs burst in a savory combination of flavors, and she couldn't hold back a sigh. She peeked at Nick. He was watching her with an inscrutable expression.

He took a bite of his own slice, before stilling. "This is delicious."

She grinned. "They have best pizza in Florida. Depending on how long you stay, you'll see Dobbs stealing a lot of it from the kitchen."

He crumpled the napkin in his hand.

For a few minutes, they ate quietly, yet it was a surprisingly comfortable silence, despite the task ahead. Once they resumed speaking, the conversation flowed nicely, as she ate enough pizza and garlic rolls for three. Perhaps she was more nervous than she realized. Was she actually going to ask a stranger to be her pretend boyfriend?

Yes, she was.

She decided to go through with it somewhere between her second slice of pizza and her third garlic roll. She opened her mouth to ask a dozen times, yet something stopped her every time.

First, it wasn't polite to ask someone to be your fake date while eating pizza.

Then, it wasn't polite to ask someone to be your fake date while eating garlic rolls.

*Finally, it wasn't polite to ask someone to be your fake date while **not** eating pizza or garlic rolls.*

A hundred excuses froze her a hundred times. Finally, she pushed her plate away, lest she start gnawing on it. And everyone knew it wasn't polite to ask someone to be your fake date while gnawing on a plate.

He smiled. "Are you full?"

She lifted a shoulder, yet in truth she was lucky she hadn't worn her slim pants. "I was full two garlic rolls ago."

"I'm glad you enjoyed it," He took the remaining slice of pizza. He'd saved the last piece in case she wanted it.

Fake Boyfriend 101, indeed.

Finally, neither food nor excuses remained between her and her fake date. Nick sat back and threaded his hands through his hair. "I had a nice time." His voice was warm, and he seemed more relaxed than in their short acquaintance. It softened him, making him even more handsome, more alluring. *More irresistible.*

"So did I." It was true. She'd enjoyed this fake date better than her last dozen real ones. Of course, technically this wasn't a fake date, or a date at all, really. It was a proposition, or it would be as soon as she could convince her mouth to cooperate. Perhaps she could begin with something innocuous, if a little forward. "We should go out again," she blurted out.

She clamped her mouth shut. That had been nearly as forward as demanding the date in the first place. His gaze turned pensive. "My situation is complicated." Regret, amidst other indecipherable emotions, flashed. "I'm only here temporarily."

Three slices of pizza and an unwise amount of garlic churned in her stomach. She wasn't proposing a real relationship, so why should it matter if he wasn't interested?

He pursed his lips together. "Yet I haven't made it this far by ignoring opportunities. I would like to see you again."

Her heart thumped relief, satisfaction and something wholly unidentifiable. She took a deep breath, plastered the widest smile she could. "How about next week?"

"Sure." He nodded. "Which day?"

"All of them."

His smile faltered. "I'm sorry?"

"What I'm asking is..." She took a deep breath. "Would you be my boyfriend?"

CHAPTER 3

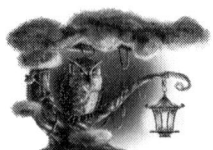

*S*he seemed like a normal woman. Smarter than average and perhaps a little eccentric, yet normal. He'd accepted her invitation to gather information, yet somewhere between the awkward entrance and savory meal, he'd begun to truly enjoy himself. She was bright, lively and witty, and she certainly knew computers.

She'd also just asked a complete stranger to be her boyfriend.

"It's not what it sounds like."

"All right," he said carefully. "Because it sounds like you just asked me to be your boyfriend."

"Perhaps it is what it sounds like."

Oh boy.

"I don't actually want you to be my boyfriend," she swiftly added. "I need a fake boyfriend."

He blinked. "That may be worse."

Twin spots of pink stained her cheeks. "I promise I have a logical explanation. I'm not the sort of woman to ask a man to be her boyfriend after a few hours." As he lowered his chin, she amended, "I'm not *usually* that sort of woman." She rubbed her forehead. "This is not going well."

He unwittingly softened. She looked so miserable, and not at all unhinged. Perhaps she had a good reason after all. "Tell me."

She looked up.

"Why do you need a fake boyfriend?"

"Really?" She blinked. At his nod, she took a deep breath. "Okay, here goes. It all started when I inadvertently told my mother…"

Dominick sat back as she wove an intricate tale of boyfriends, anniversaries, families and expectations. It sounded fantastic at first, yet right around the description of her mother's letter, something familiar surfaced. The need to not disappoint, to give your family a present of peace and joy. The need for mothers to see their children settled and happy. If she was unhinged, then he was as well, for her plan traveled from crazy to outlandish to not entirely illogical. He could even understand why she chose him, a stranger who would soon leave, instead of one of the men at the office.

When she finished, her cheeks were pink, her eyes uncertain. He resisted the urge to caress the worry from her. "You're speechless." She chewed her bottom lip. "Please tell me I didn't break you."

He smiled softly. "You didn't break me. You merely surprised me."

"In an I'm-getting-a-restraining-order sort of way?"

He chuckled lowly. "No, in a my-family-is-just-as-eccentric kind of way."

She scrunched up her nose. "In a you're-considering-it sort of way?"

Was he actually considering it? It sounded crazy, yet she drew him in, and the thought of spending an entire week with her tempted him like a double fudge sundae after a sugar-free year. When he'd discreetly asked several colleagues about her, a few showed clear interest.

He'd somehow managed not to fire them on the spot.

Perhaps this could be an opportunity, a chance to discover more about the office. Most of the employees had been reluctant to talk to him, hinting he could be fired before his first paycheck if he persisted. Apparently, any signs of dissension were met with a swift farewell.

That was not the Knight Technology he created.

Dobbs was a problem, and clearly not the only one, signaling a much greater issue in the chain of command. He couldn't fix it unless he learned more, and a trip away from the office with a long-term employee could be very enlightening.

The waitress came by and dropped the check on the table. Adrianna was fast. He was *faster*. He snatched the bill, glanced at the ridiculously small total and set out the cash, including a generous tip. He handed it to the waitress. "We're all set."

Adrianna folded her arms across her chest. "I'd like to pay. After all, I'm the one who asked you out."

"Yes, you did," he agreed. "However, a man likes to treat his girlfriend." As pink lips parted, he winked. "At least you don't have to worry about being the only eccentric."

She leapt up with such pure radiance, he would have given her the moon had she asked. Then... she hugged him.

Attraction. Desire. A feeling of utter rightness. Satisfaction surged, as he embraced the petite woman. She fit perfectly in his arms, all delicious warmth and generous curves. Yet something beyond the physical sparked, something raw and instinctual, at this vibrant woman who commanded pure sunshine.

"I'm sorry." She edged back. "I was just so excited. I didn't mean to, you know, um..."

Distort his senses? Distract him from his mission? Make him wonder, *What if?*

Did he have to let her go? Something in him demanded he keep her, to hold on to this treasure he'd found. He couldn't do that – at least not yet. With physical effort, he opened his arms, and she edged back.

"Please tell me you haven't moved from a this-is-crazy-but-I-have-nothing-better-to-do-so-why-not stance to a maybe-a-restraining-order-isn't-such-a-bad-idea stance."

He chuckled softly, resisted the urge to grasp her once more. "Don't worry. I have a my-family-hugs-all-the-time stance." And then, either because he couldn't resist or simply didn't want to, he touched her shoulder. "If we're going to pretend to be boyfriend and girlfriend, we'll have to get used to hugging."

Actually, they would have to get used to far more than that.

If the thought brought more satisfaction than he anticipated, he didn't mention it.

༄

ADRIANNA CHECKED the next item on her *Fake Date* list. "What do you like to do?"

"Do you mean beyond computers?"

"Yes."

"More computers."

Adrianna shifted on the luxurious seat of Nick's late model hybrid. She assumed she would drive to her parents' house, or they would take separate cars, but he was insistent he drive. She also hadn't expected the plush seats that made her never want to rise or the electronics that talked like the car from that TV show she watched as a kid.

The days leading to the trip had passed swiftly, as they

prepared, both mentally and logistically. The day after their pizza date, he'd asked if she wanted to have dinner again. She agreed, so they could go over the role, of course.

The day after that, he asked if she wanted to meet for coffee.

After that, it was bowling.

The next day, the movies.

By their fifth "research session," a trip to a nearby park for a picnic, the excuse had been well used. But each visit was enjoyable, and she learned at least something about her fake boyfriend every time. Still, the feeling he was hiding something never quite disappeared, with his vague answers and surreptitious glances.

"What did you tell them I liked?" His question brought her back to the present. "I'm sure we can find a way to explain it, just like with the name. How did they take it when you told them I now go by my middle name?"

"Mom was surprised, but it couldn't be helped." She shrugged. "With all our pretending, I didn't want you to have to assume a fake name also."

For the briefest of moments, his eyes shuttered. Yet another peculiarity, like how someone that skilled with computers worked as a temp, or how he changed the subject every time she asked about work. "You must have some hobbies."

"I have been known to act." He winked. "I'm currently playing a pretend boyfriend."

"You don't say." She grinned. "What other parts have you played?"

"Well." He thumped the steering wheel. "I was a pretend trapeze artist, but that didn't end well. The pretend lion tamer position was a veritable disaster."

She chuckled. "Have you played a pretend hairdresser?"

"Ah yes. Lovely for me, not so much for the client." They

both smiled, as he expertly guided the car around a large tractor-trailer. "In addition to my pretend jobs, I like to be physically active. Even when my schedule is hectic, I exercise every day."

"That's obvious." She closed her eyes, opened them. "Did I say that out loud?"

His widened smile betrayed the answer. "You did."

She couldn't help herself. She'd touched those muscles several times when she accidentally bumped into him. All right, several *dozen* times, and the accidents may not have been accidents, but it was his fault for being so attractive. "Clearly, hearing things is something else you do," she teased. "Anything else?"

He sat back. "I like to cook."

Her heart fluttered. Some women preferred bad boys, while others liked heartthrobs. A guy who could cook? *Yum.* "What do you like to cook?"

"Really anything. My grandparents owned a restaurant, and at one point I even considered becoming a chef. If you'd like, I can cook for you sometime."

Was it getting hot in here? She cleared her throat. "I'd love that. Once we return, we can make it a date."

He frowned and said nothing. Ah yes, he was leaving soon after they returned. Something acidic churned in her stomach. "I'm afraid I'm not much of a cook. I am, however, excellent at setting things on fire."

He gave her a sideways look. "I don't believe it."

"Believe it. I set toast on fire twice. I made brownies sizzle. And do you have any idea how much smoke cereal can produce?"

He laughed. "How is that even possible?"

"I was trying to make that dessert with cereal and marshmallows, and I seriously overestimated the cooking time. The good news is no one expects me to bring anything to these get-togethers. I will, however, have a line of laptops and other assorted electronics ready for me to fix."

His eyes lit up. "I can help you with that. And I'm happy to cook for you anytime."

The traffic slowed as they neared a service station. Nick changed to the right lane and flipped on his signal. "This is the last rest area before we leave the highway. Why don't we stop here?" He pulled onto the exit and entered the lot, parking next to a large, chartered bus. She grasped her purse and undid her seatbelt, but before she could open the door, he came around and opened it for her. He held out his hand.

A chef, computer lover and chivalrous gentleman?

She needed a cold shower.

Adrianna settled for washing her hands with cold water in the ladies' room. She used a paper towel to wipe her neck, shivering as the cool water chilled heated skin. She had to keep it together. Her inner conscience reminded her that if she was truly together, she wouldn't be bringing a fake date home. She reminded her conscience that Nick was excessively hot. Her conscience agreed.

By the time she returned, Nick was already there, leaning his excessively hot body against the gleaming car. He held the door for her, yet when she slid her seatbelt out, he stopped her with a hand on her wrist. "There's something we should do before we reach our destination."

She released the latch, and it retreated with a gentle whir. "Get our heads examined?"

"Not a bad idea, but no." He leaned forward. "I was thinking something a little more intimate."

Something intimate?

Yes, please. Yes, please. Yes, please. Yes, please. Yes, please. Yes, please. Yes, please. Yes, please. Yes, please. Yes, please. Yes, please. Yes, please. Yes, please. Yes, please. Yes, please. Yes, please. Yes, please. Yes, please. Yes, please. Yes, please.

"What did you have in mind?"

"I'm referring to a kiss, of course."

Yes, please.

Could he sense her desire? Her attraction? Sapphire eyes betrayed no secrets. "Your family isn't going to believe we're in a relationship if we act like we barely know each other. It's going to be a little awkward, and obvious, if we share our first kiss there."

He was right. It would be talked about for years, gossiped about on every phone conversation, detailed in letters around the globe. She licked dry lips and shifted her gaze. His lips were full and sensual, amidst chiseled features. "So when did you want to…" She waved her hand. "You know?"

A tinge of amusement flashed, tinted with a dash of satisfaction. "We can't do it while we're there."

"Of course not."

"We're going straight there."

"True."

"How about now?"

She froze.

Approximately a year and a half passed. "Now? Now. Now?" *How many times had she said now?* "Of course. That's a great idea. Perfect. Now." Her voice was so high-pitched it sounded like she had sucked all the helium out of a carnival balloon. She cleared her throat, lowered her voice. "Ready?"

Great. Now she resembled an *oboe*.

He had her flustered already, and they hadn't even brushed lips. "It seems like an opportune time. No one is around." They had parked a distance from the rest area, far from the bustling families and strolling tourists with their noses buried in their smartphones. A sea of empty parking spaces surrounded them, with one empty bus the only company.

Yet instead of triumph, his expression turned serious. "We don't have to do this. If you'd rather, we can deal with matters as they arise."

Perhaps, except her parents would not merely tolerate a kiss, they would expect it. "I want to do this."

Something sparked in his eyes, a nameless emotion so light and swift, it was gone in an instant. When he spoke his voice was low, somber. "Anytime you want to stop, just say the word. You are in control."

Then why did it feel like he held all the power? Yet she nodded, playing the part she had assigned herself, perfectly still as he edged closer.

And closer…

And closer…

Then he pressed his lips to hers.

The world melted away.

Every doubt vanished, uncertainty and hesitation disappearing amidst passion's whisper. His lips were tender, gentle, caressing. Firm and pliant, warm and oh-so-bold. He smelled like oak and spice and just a hint of chocolate. He edged closer.

The spark turned into an inferno.

She moaned her surrender, closing heavy eyes as heat surrounded her. He was hardness defined, sculpted muscles and unrelenting strength. The darkness held fireworks, as she moved in a world of endless sensation. She brushed against his broad chest, electrifying every part of her body.

Thoughts scattered, as he deepened the kiss. He demanded surrender, yet she seized her own power. Passion took control, as they kissed again and again, on lips, on necks, peppering burning skin. She gasped, pressed closer. It was not enough. She needed more…

A bang shook the entire car.

They broke away, and for a moment, the world teetered in a passion-filled haze. She closed her eyes, fought for strength.

What just happened?

As the banging sounded again, she opened her eyes and gasped. A man stood outside their window, uniformed and badged, and he wasn't alone. Two dozen retirees stood frozen, wearing expressions ranging from astonishment to annoyance to unabashed delight, in front of a bus with four glaring words:

Sunny Trails Retirement Home.

Somehow Nick maintained complete control as he rolled down the window, nodded to the policeman.

"ID and registration."

Perfect. Instead of visiting her family with a fake date, she was going to jail. Yet would it really be worse? Perhaps she should tell the cop they had robbed a bank during the drive.

The sheriff took both of their IDs. After a moment he returned hers, but he kept Nick's tightly clutched in his gloved hand. He looked at Nick, then back at the ID, then at Nick again.

And for the first time, her partner looked uncomfortable.

She frowned, as the officer peered closer. "Is this really you?"

Nick visibly tightened. "Yes, it is."

"Wow."

A single word, a thousand implications and one question:

Who was Nick Walters?

CHAPTER 4

The cop recognized him.
    Dominick had seen it enough times. First came confusion, then skepticism and finally excitement. It was bad enough when he'd been splashed across the Internet as one of the youngest self-made billionaires in the world. Yet when his book hit every bestseller list, his popularity launched into the stratosphere. He'd written it on a whim, a motivational tome touching on far more than computers and business, yet readers had related to his tenacious climb. He'd sold millions.

He'd left the eyeglasses back in Miami, figuring the beard and clothing would be enough of a disguise when not in the office. Judging by the cop's somber look, clearly it had been a mistake. "Please tell me this isn't what it looks like."

"Of course not, officer," Adrianna swiftly broke in, her suspicion-filled eyes pinned to his. "We aren't even together."

The officer's expression darkened. Somewhere in the back, an octogenarian giggled.

"What she's trying to say is our relationship is complicated," Dominick grasped her hand. "We're still defining it, but of course we're together. She's a beautiful woman, and I got carried away. I'm sorry."

"We don't mind!" a silver haired lady with a bright smile and sparkling eyes exclaimed.

"Please continue." Another grinned wildly.

"Does anyone have popcorn?" a third called.

Matters were deteriorating by the moment.

The worst part was he couldn't regret the kiss. It may have started as "practice," yet it quickly delved into something far more substantial, infinitely more intense. Something sparked when their lips met. Passion and fire, a sensual onslaught. Yet it was more than physical desire, more than basic need. It just seemed right.

Yet the consequences were alarming:

The spectators were smiling in glee.

The officer was fingering his handcuffs.

Adrianna folded her arms across her chest.

He cringed. "I really am sorry, officer."

The officer looked at him for a moment more, before breaking into a smile. "I can't say it hasn't happened to me once or twice. Next time, go somewhere a little more private."

Dominick let out a breath of relief. "Will do." The officer handed him back his license, and the audience departed, some with audible groans. Silently, Dominick raised his window and started the car.

His passenger said nothing as they drove out of the parking lot and back onto the highway. The silence continued as they drove the first mile, and then the next five. Finally, just after they glided through the toll booth express lane, Adrianna said quietly, "What did the officer mean back there?"

His hands tightened on the butter leather wheel. "I'm sorry?"

"When he asked if it was really you." Her scrutiny burned hot against his neck. "It was almost like he recognized you."

Not good. He forced a grin. "That's impossible. I haven't been on the cover of *Mastermind Criminals Quarterly* since July." He had, however, been featured on CNN, among a dozen other news websites and channels.

She laughed, but it resonated as falsely as his smile. "Why would he ask something like that?"

"There could be many reasons." *The main one being he was a celebrity in disguise.* "Perhaps he didn't think I looked like my picture. Maybe he thought I had a fake ID, which I don't." He kept his eyes on the road, switching into cruise control. "What else could it be?"

She studied him for a moment, then lifted her chin. "I have an idea. Show me your driver's license, and I'll tell you if it looks like you."

"Absolutely not."

She gaped, as he bit back an oath. Obviously, he couldn't show her a driver's license with his real name, yet he hadn't planned on being so adamant. "I'm sorry. It's just if you see it, you may think differently of me." True, yet not for any reason she'd ever imagine.

"It can't be that bad." As expected, she misinterpreted the motive behind his protest. "I'll show you mine if you show me yours." She sucked in a breath of air. "You know what I meant. I wasn't referring to... to..."

This time his smile was genuine. "What exactly were you—"

"Don't you dare finish that sentence, Nick Walters." She crossed her arms over her chest, but her eyes sparkled. "Now you have to say yes."

He sobered immediately. "I'm afraid not. It's just a little too... shocking."

She was silent for a moment. "That bad, huh?" The words

were said lightly, yet an edge tinged them. "Perhaps one day you'll trust me."

Perhaps one day he would. She asked no more, yet he did not mistake her silence for acceptance.

Did she suspect he was not as he seemed?

⚜

"Everything will be fine."
That was a lie.
"All will go smoothly."
That was another lie.
"Everyone will believe exactly what we tell them."
Gimme an L! Gimme an I! Gimme an E!

Adrianna rubbed the bridge of her nose. Pretended she was somewhere other than the front porch of her parents' white stucco ranch home, poised to fool her entire family into thinking she had a boyfriend. How had this seemed like a good idea?

A boyfriend with secrets of his own. His response when she asked to see his driver's license had been downright suspicious. Was he hiding something? She would consider the query later, if she somehow survived this week.

"Are you all right? You look a little freaked out."

"That's wonderful," she said cheerily. "Because I am a lot freaked out." *Breathe.* "But I'm sure it'll be fine."

He looked at her skeptically. "Are you trying to convince me or yourself?"

"Both really."

As his gaze softened, she relaxed. He grasped her hand, and all calmness fled. His large hand eclipsed her small one, as he held her firmly, almost *possessively*.

The door opened.

"He's here!"

"It's fantastic to meet you!"

"We've been waiting all month!"

It was like a tornado. Or a stampede. Or a shark frenzy. Or perhaps a stampede of sharks in a tornado. Two sets of grandparents, four aunts, three uncles and an assortment of cousins of all ages surged forward, their arms opened wide, their smiles wider. They shook hands, patted backs, kissed cheeks and gave all sorts of assorted greetings appropriate if one were seeing a close relative after a year-long separation. A perfect stranger – not so much.

She squeezed her eyes shut, opened them to an empty porch.

That could have gone better.

Adrianna rushed into the house. Right now her mother was probably asking Nick how many children he wanted. Then she would ask what names he'd picked out, before suggesting they name their firstborn after her great aunt. Finally, she would show him the clothing she had already bought for the child named after her great aunt.

She needed to save him.

The tornado had calmed from an F5 to an F1, yet the room was still electric with movement. Clearly, she had turned invisible, as no one noticed, mentioned or otherwise detected her arrival in the large dining room with its huge oak table, three side tables and enough folding chairs for a small city. Nick was perched at the head of the table on the *throne*, a massive, gilded chair they had inherited from the same great aunt who would likely be her child's namesake. He was staring at her mother.

"Don't be shy. How many do you want?"

Oh. My. Goodness.

She lunged forward. "Mom, that isn't something you should be asking!"

Everyone turned to her.

She wasn't invisible after all.

This fact was made inexplicably clear as the masses descended. There were bear hugs and gentle embraces, pecks on the cheek and wet smacks on the forehead, which then required a rubbing thumb to get rid of the resulting lipstick smear. Questions abound, about her work, social life, eating habits and more. For a group of people who agreed on nothing, they all agreed that her eating habits were atrocious. There were smiles and clucking and a lot of advice.

Yet despite the chaos, she loved it.

Because she loved every single one of them.

"Now please explain why I shouldn't be asking how many he wants." Her mother, now suddenly as calm as the Dead Sea, waited expectantly.

She stepped towards him, yet couldn't make it through the mob of relatives surrounding him. Personal space was not a relevant concept in her home. "It's just not appropriate."

Her entire family sported matching frowns. "Why not?"

"Because–" She pushed forward, gained approximately half an inch. "He's not thinking about that now."

"When should he think about it?"

This conversation was getting stranger by the minute. "I don't know. A few years."

Her mother parted her lips. "You want me to ask him how many matzo balls he wants in his soup in a few years?"

Matzo balls?

Oh, darn. Oh darn. Oh darn. Oh, darn. Oh darn. Oh darn. Oh, darn. Oh darn. Oh darn. Oh, darn. Oh darn. Oh darn. Oh darn. Oh, darn. Oh darn. Oh darn. Oh, darn. Oh darn. Oh darn. Oh darn. Oh, darn. Oh darn. Oh darn. Oh, darn. Oh darn.

She closed her eyes. Wished herself invisible. Failed.

She opened them to find her family staring at her as if she

was one matzo ball short of a soup bowl. Nick's lips twitched. "You think I should wait years to decide on the number of matzo balls?"

How did a man's voice sound so yummy? Forget the matzo balls. He was more delicious than sweet wine. "I... I... think it's a very important decision that requires serious contemplation."

He grinned. Her entire family looked at him. Looked at her. At him. At her. She'd bet a week's salary each and every one of them was deciding what to wear to their wedding.

He stretched out his long legs, a natural king of his domain. "Perhaps you are right. Imagine the consequences if I ate an extra matzo ball, or one too few."

"Yes, imagine," she drawled. "The ramifications would last for years."

"Indeed." His smile widened, as he gestured to the ladle in her mother's hands. "Yet, I am going to risk it. I'll take three."

Oh dear.

The rest of the family looked on in approval, as her beaming mother plopped three plump matzo balls into the soup with a splash. They bobbed on top of the swirling amber concentrate, casting the warm scent of her grandmother's recipe throughout the room. Tense muscles softened at memories of blissful holidays and joyous family dinners. Her mother's soup made everything a little better.

Nick sighed appreciatively. "I haven't had a home-cooked meal in months."

It was the wrong thing to say. Her father winced, and the rest of her family looked on with surprise and pity. Her mother?

She looked like she'd just won the $18 bingo jackpot.

She clapped her hands together. "It's lucky I prepared light refreshments."

Nick's eyes lit as he held up the bowl. "This is perfect."

"The soup?" Her mother laughed. "That's just the starter before the appetizers. Aunt Mabel!"

"I'm sorry, did you say *before* the appet–"

Any comments were immediately and completely overwhelmed by a bevy of movement. Like a general with her soldiers, her mother directed a regiment of relatives in and out of the kitchen, as they brought out enough food to feed not only an army, but the opposing forces and three or four more armies, just in case they happened to show up.

Nick's eyes grew as wide as the parade of platters, each in its own colorful ceramic dish gifted from decades of weddings, holidays and other assorted celebrations. It included a steaming vegetable lasagna, cheese covered mashed potatoes, homemade biscuits and about a thousand or so other dishes.

As Dominick stared wide-eyed at the food, Adrianna considered her options:

A. Yell "An alligator is eating the matzo ball soup!" and run out of the house.

B. Yell "An alligator is eating the biscuits!" and run out of the house.

C. Yell "An alligator is eating the mashed potatoes!" and run out of the house.

Her mother gave her a sideways look and positioned herself in front of the door leading out of the house.

Her options disappeared like Aunt Mabel's jelly-filled doughnuts on Sunday morning.

Nick looked as if he were considering the same options, yet instead of yelling a random predator, he grinned. "It looks delicious."

His smile was warm and genuine, and his eyes crinkled at the corners. And suddenly, an altogether different type of discomfort rose.

Desire.

Right in the middle of her mother's dining room, surrounded by dozens of relatives, the world melted away. The tangle of aromas faded into the distance, as did her family, and all other sights and sounds. Every sensation honed on a single man.

Nick.

He was beyond handsome, gorgeous even, with his dark hair, sensual features. She fought the urge to see if he was as gifted a kisser as she remembered. Yet far more than his handsome visage drew her – the intelligence burning in those sapphire eyes, the humor that quirked up the sides of his lips, the kindness he'd shown her family. With this man, the inside was just as sexy as the outside.

Mesmerized, she couldn't even hear her family's conversation. Or actually… She blinked as reality returned, as every single person silently stared at them. Her mother hadn't smiled this widely since she won third place in the spelling bee. As if the mute button finally deactivated, conversation started once more, with a concoction of hushed whispers and tinkling laughter that concealed no secrets.

This was bad.

She managed to relax slightly as Nick accepted a plate from her mother. He took a small portion of every dish, building a hill and then a small mountain. Finally, he sat down, not seeming to mind that he played performer in a one-person play. Everyone watched eagerly as he took his first bite, then announced, "This is delicious."

Her mother clapped. "If this isn't enough, just wait for the anniversary party."

Was it too late to yell, "Alligator?"

"I HOPE THIS WILL DO." Mrs. Lewis smiled widely at him. "We use it as an office, but it's my son's old bedroom."

Dominick returned the grin, which made hers widen more. As a semi-celebrity and billionaire business owner, he was accustomed to attention, yet he'd never felt as celebrated as Adrianna's boyfriend.

What would they do if they discovered the truth?

He pushed the uncomfortable thought aside as he stepped into the room. More childhood room than office, it contained an old homemade computer, posters of nineties sci-fi films and an entire wall of trophies from half a dozen little league teams.

Mrs. Lewis lingered at the old trophies. "Joshua always excelled in school and sports, as did Adrianna. A mother couldn't be prouder." She picked up a picture of a little boy and girl at the beach, next to a younger version of herself. Her gaze softened, as she peered twenty years into the past. "Don't tell Adrianna, but a part of me still sees them as my babies."

He gave a soft smile. "I won't say a word."

She replaced the picture on the dresser. "Joshua will be here at the end of the week, but you won't have to worry about moving. He and his wife have five kids, so they use the guest house by the lake. Want to see a couple of pictures?" She didn't wait for him to reply before whipping out a couple of picture *albums*. Yet as she showed him numerous grandkids, sharing everything from science fair wins to second grade hobbies, it actually felt kind of nice. It reminded him of home.

Finally, she shut the book. "I'd better check on Adrianna to see if she's done fixing my laptop. Tomorrow there will be a long line, so I always sneak mine in first." She winked. "I'm so glad you found each other. The way you look at each other… I can tell it's something special."

Dominick said nothing as Mrs. Lewis walked out of the room, then sank on the springy bed. She was wrong, of course. He'd just met Adrianna a few days ago. She didn't even know his real name, or that he was actually the billionaire CEO of Knight Technology. It was impossible.

Yet a voice whispered, *Just perhaps...*

"Are you feeling all right?"

Dominick stood as Adrianna slipped through the door of their adjoining bedrooms. "I'm fine."

"Are you sure?" She eyed him dubiously. "You didn't have to eat everything."

"I couldn't let them down after they worked so hard. Plus, it truly was delicious." If only there hadn't been so much of it. "As an added benefit, I can now hibernate for the winter."

She chuckled. "You really haven't had a home-cooked meal in months?" Her face turned crimson. "I'm sorry, that's none of my business."

Even he had been surprised to realize how long it had been. He'd gifted his parents with an around-the-world cruise, but as soon as they returned, he would visit. "I don't mind that you asked." And strangely, he didn't. As his life had delved further and further into the public realm, the desire to stay private had soared. Yet somehow with her, it didn't matter. "I've been busy with work."

Suspicion flashed in her eyes. Why had he mentioned work again? "As you know, a criminal enterprise takes a lot of time to run," he added.

"How would I know?" Her eyes sparkled. "You're the criminal."

He fashioned a look of mock somberness. "The police almost arrested us both."

She grinned, yet it faded as she scrutinized him. Was she remembering every time he'd nearly betrayed the truth? He needed a distraction. "As I recall, we never did finish practicing."

"No, we didn't." She licked her lips, and suddenly, *he* was distracted. "We should probably remedy that."

"An excellent idea." He edged closer.

"Yes, it is." So did she.

They met in the middle. He dipped his head down, brushing her lips. Her lips were soft and pliant, and tasted like strawberries and newfound opportunities. He breathed in the scent of gardenias as he pressed closer, bringing her flush against him. She was all beautiful curves, petite to his far larger size, and yet somehow she fit perfectly against him, as if she belonged there.

As if she belonged to him.

A sense of utter rightness surged, desire and need and something far more elemental. The need to be with this woman, to *keep* this woman. Possessiveness consumed him, as something ignited. He may claim it was about distraction or practicing, yet the truth burned.

They were just getting started.

CHAPTER 5

The sun streamed across the wide porch, its warm rays illuminating the world in amber brilliance. Adrianna stretched taut muscles, lunging with one leg and then the next, reaching up to stretch her arms. The supple fabric molded to her, its wicking surface already lapping up moisture in the heated day. Yet nothing was as heated as the man next to her.

How could she not have noticed him the moment he walked into the office? He truly was massive, his build towering, his chest broad and firm. His face was an artist's masterpiece, his indigo eyes sparkling with intelligence and just a little bit of mischievousness. His thick hair had been combed neatly back, yet a lock escaped on his forehead. The urge to sweep it back was almost irresistible.

"Do you mind if I take my shirt off?"

Oh. My. Goodness.

"That would be great."

Um, what did she just say?

"I mean I would really enjoy it."

Oh dear.

"I mean you should be comfortable. The less clothing, the better, right?"

Lost: Her good sense. Please call if found. Reward.

She opened her eyes to a hunk of a man staring at her with a broad smile. "Go for it," she said weakly.

He reached down and lifted his shirt, revealing the man equivalent of a quadruple scoop sundae covered in hot fudge, caramel, sprinkles and forty-five cherries. His chest was broad and muscled, his abs defined, his biceps bulging with power. Her gaze lowered…

"Are you sure you want to jog?"

Nope. She wanted to stay here and watch him. While eating a quadruple scoop sundae covered in hot fudge–

"Adrianna?"

"Yes? Yes!" Heat bloomed from her neck all the way down her body, culminating in some very interesting spots. She was hot. And bothered. Both, really, and it had nothing to do with the exercise she hadn't started and everything to do with the man-sized sundae before her.

And just like that, she imagined him covered in chocolate, smothered in caramel and sprinkled in–

"Are you ready for our jog?"

"Yes!" She blushed. "I mean, yes, thank you." It seemed like a good idea when he first suggested it. After all, they both enjoyed physical activity and the outdoors. It would give them a little break from the family, and show they enjoyed being with each other. Yet she had forgotten how attractive he was. Hopefully, she didn't run into a car. "I'm ready if you are," she lied.

"Let's go."

Somehow she managed not to run into a car. She did run into *him* when he paused at an intersection. Then again when he stopped to let someone pass. And once more when he halted to drink water.

Okay, so maybe she did it on purpose.

But who could blame her? He was always attractive, but now he was sizzling hot, literally and metaphorically, his muscles straining and sheening in the sun. The clothing stuck to him like a second skin, outlining corded definition and firm muscles. He was as hard as steel.

He didn't comment as she repeatedly bumped into him, just like she didn't comment when his hands lingered a tad longer than necessary to steady her when she paused at the intersection. Then again when she let someone pass and again when she drank water.

Yeah, two were definitely playing this game.

Finally, they made it back to her parents' home, where her mother emerged with two tall glasses of lemonade. "Did you have fun?"

Oh yes. Inappropriate, unwise, all-too-tempting fun. As if she understood her wayward thoughts, her mother winked. She handed them the glasses. "You guys look hot. I can't believe it's eighty degrees in December."

While he sipped his drink, Adrianna gulped the sweet liquid. Nick reached out and stilled her hand. "Be careful. You'll give yourself a stomachache." She swallowed slower, yet her heart beat faster. It was almost like he was a real boyfriend, taking care of the woman he loved.

Her mother beamed. "I know what will cool you off."

Oh. No. There could be only one activity her mother meant, and it involved even less clothing than jogging. "Mother–"

"Swimming." Her mother clapped her hands. "With this warm weather, the pool is delightful."

Running next to a shirtless Nick: a challenge. Swimming with even less clothing? A very bad idea.

Or a very good idea, her traitorous body protested. *And while they were at it, why wear clothing at all?*

"I can't go! I– I didn't pack a swimsuit!" Thank goodness for her forgetfulness. "I mean, it's too bad, but I can't swim in this."

Was that disappointment in Nick's eyes? Her mother pursed her lips, undoubtedly calculating every possible solution with the tenacity of a soldier. "You can just take it off."

Well, that was unexpected.

She had nothing to respond to that, and neither did Nick, who was gazing at her with the look of a man who'd been attacked by a lion and won the same lottery at the same time. Or perhaps he was the lion, the powerful predator. Was she the prey? "Mother!"

"I didn't mean you should swim in your undergarments." Her mother waved her hand. "I'm sure we can find something. What about you, Nick?"

Nick ran a hand through his hair, tightening his biceps. Perhaps swimming in the nude wasn't such a bad idea. Of course, if she was going to be naked, it would only be fair that he–

No. This was exactly why this was a bad idea. She was one muscle flex away from plopping down a lawn chair, grabbing some popcorn and drooling.

"A swim sounds great." He rubbed his hands together. "I don't have a suit, but I can just wear these shorts."

"I'd be happy to wash them for you afterwards," her mother offered helpfully. She nodded to Adrianna. "You can use one of your old swimsuits."

"That's not a good ide–"

"It's the perfect solution." Her mother happily ignored her. "I saw one of your suits in your room."

The clothing in her childhood room was ten years, four thousand tacos and ten thousand ice cream sundaes ago. There was a reason she'd left them behind. "It probably doesn't fit."

"Of course, it fits." Her mother propelled her towards her room. "Now run off and get dressed."

And just like that, she found herself in her room, staring at a pale pink dresser with unicorn-shaped handles. She opened the drawer...

"Oh crap."

CONTROL FUELED HIS SUCCESS. It was what made Dominick a billionaire before the age of thirty, forging a company with hard work, passion and a dream. It was what put him on the cover of countless business magazines, allowed him to build an international juggernaut and write a bestseller that touched millions. Yet watching Adrianna emerge in the fabric scraps masquerading as a bikini?

That tested his control like nothing else.

It was made of string. Oh, there were other parts, too. Officially it covered the necessary bits, barely. When she sauntered in that teeny, tiny yellow bikini (and yes, it was polka-dotted), he did what any strong, self-assured, confident man would do:

He stared. Then he stared some more. And proceeded to stare.

He didn't mean to, of course. It was rather unseemly. But the bikini was way too small, and Adrianna was way too...

Beautiful. Lovely. Exquisite. Perfect. *Oh-so-tempting.*

She was desire itself, flawless with curves that made a man's mouth water. Her skin was creamy pinkness, lovely features highlighted by a waterfall of silky black hair. Generous breasts overfilled the two triangles, leading down to a trim waist, before flaring to curvy hips and firm legs. Her toes were painted pink with sparkles.

She stopped directly in front of him, folded her arms across her chest. It lifted... *everything.*

"Are you all right?" Her voice emerged breathless.

"Of course." His own voice emerged like a seventh grader on the verge of puberty. He cleared his throat, deepened it. "Of course." And then, just because he couldn't not, he murmured, "You're beautiful."

She flushed, yet a hint of pleasure sparked. "Ready to go in the water?"

Yes, he was.

The water was a shock of cold, yet as delightful as Mrs. Lewis predicted. The sun's sweltering heat instantly lessened as the coolness surrounded him, as he drifted in blissful weightlessness. Even Adrianna's features relaxed. "This feels good," she admitted.

"It does." He leaned back and eased his body, lying in a floating position. He bobbed gently up and down... until a tsunami hit.

He stood instantly, shaking himself like a dog in a rain shower. Looked at the woman sitting primly on the stairs, her expression the picture of feigned innocence. "Did you just splash me?"

"Nope." Her lips twitched.

"Really?" He walked along the bottom of the pool, folded his arms as he emerged into the shallow side. "Because I distinctly felt a splash."

"Did you?" She choked back a laugh. "Are you certain?"

He looked down at his waterlogged form. "Fairly certain."

"It must have been someone else." She tapped her chin. "Or perhaps something else. As you know, there are alligators in Florida."

He chuckled lowly, edging into her space. "Admit it was you."

She lifted her chin. The sunlight glinted off cat green

eyes, and her hair sparkled like glittering onyx. "All right, I admit it. You just lost the splashing contest."

She was adorable. "You didn't tell me we were having a splashing contest."

"Ignorance of the game doesn't mean you can't lose." She stuck her cute little nose in the air. "So you lost."

"Did I?" he murmured. "I'd like a rematch."

"A rematch? Why not? I'm sure I can–"

He didn't let her finish. He splashed her beautiful form, careful not to be too forceful, even as he drenched her. She stared at him, her mouth agape, her entire body glistening with diamond droplets. The urge to smooth them was almost irresistible.

"You're in trouble now," she growled playfully. "I'm a gold medal winner in competitive splashing."

Digging her hands into the liquid weaponry, she deluged him with half the Atlantic, even as he returned her volleys. Back and forth, simultaneously and endlessly, they splashed, filling the air with moisture, and the world with explosive booms. Finally, he held up his hands. "You win."

"All right!" She pumped her fist in the air, as exuberant as any Olympic champion and as breathtaking as any beauty queen. She lifted her shoulder cheekily. "So what do I win?"

"Win?" He rubbed his hands together. "What was the bet?"

"A new car or a two-week vacation in Hawaii?" she teased. "How about a million dollars?"

"Why not?" The urge to give her all that and more surged. What would she say if she knew he could easily afford it?

Her twinkling laughter proved she had no clue. She came up to him, splashing him again in her wake. "I suppose a luxury car might be a bit much to ask."

Not really. He'd spent less on a Tuesday afternoon. "What else do you want?"

She wet her lips, and looked up and down his body. This

time, he couldn't stop himself from moving closer. "Do you want something from me?" he murmured.

She gave the slightest nod.

"A kiss?"

Another nod, so slight it was barely perceptible.

He couldn't deny the winner.

He pressed his lips to hers, ever-so-softly. Yet she pushed into the kiss, molding that lithe, curvy body into him. She tasted like chocolate, sunshine and pure bliss. Emotion surged, desire, longing and so much more. Happiness, satisfaction, *possessiveness*.

He wanted this woman like none ever before. He held her nearly naked body along his length, softness to hardness, bare skin to bare skin. She was so petite and so curvy, and she fit against him in pure perfection.

And as they kissed in that sun-splashed pool, where coolness and heat swirled, something changed. All at once, their relationship didn't seem so pretend. It brought a million unnamed emotions and a single question:

What if he never let her go?

CHAPTER 6

The sound of laughter woke her.
Still in the throes of a dream that involved a certain muscular man, a lot of water and not a lot of clothing, Adrianna shifted on the taut percale sheets, stretching muscles sore from yesterday's activities. She opened heavy eyelids to a room brilliant with sunlight, illuminating unicorn and rainbow curtains and matching wallpaper in golden amber. The sun was already high in the sky, surrounded by nothing but blue, with the promise of a gorgeous day.

She breathed in sweet air, scented with her mother's savory cooking. A unicorn-shaped clock showed it was well past her normal rising time, the sounds of distant conversation confirming her leisurely morning. She jumped out of bed, too quickly as sore muscles tinged, then moved slower as she donned a light yellow sundress and brushed her hair. Finishing the rest of her routine, she departed her room and strode to the dining room.

A dozen platters stood at the sideboard, gleaming silver with thick blueberry pancakes, crispy hash browns and

French toast made from homemade challah, covered in creamy butter and powdered sugar. It smelled like heaven and home, yet despite the display, the table was empty save for one place setting. "Is anyone here?"

"There you are, sleepyhead." Her mother emerged from the kitchen, wearing a bright yellow apron that said, "Proudest. Mom. Ever." and an even brighter smile, and placed a hot cup of coffee in front of her, prepared just as she liked. "Everyone else already ate. We were shocked you weren't here, since you're usually the first up."

Her stomach growling its approval, Adrianna grasped the silvery tongs. "It must have been all the physical activity." Or a delectable man who occupied more and more of her time. He didn't leave her mind as she filled her plate, or as she sat to eat, while dodging probing questions from her mother that stopped just short of a guest list for her wedding.

Adrianna took a bite of the savory French toast, moaning lightly at the soft, sugar-covered masterpiece. Yet even as she enjoyed the fare, unease surfaced. The mystery surrounding Nick deepened with every secret he tried to distract away with clever jokes and witty repartee. Of course, he wasn't a criminal mastermind, yet increasingly frequent slips betrayed the secrets he hid.

She ate the meal quickly, then cleaned her dishes and travelled through the house, chasing the sounds of lively conversation and laughter. She emerged into the spacious living room, where a crowd had gathered around Nick and a row of computers queued in line like at an Orlando theme park. "Good morning." She smiled.

Nick was typing furiously on her father's laptop, an old device beleaguered by a vicious virus. That he would help her family came as no surprise, yet this time he would not be successful. She had done everything possible to save the dinosaur device, and was now searching for the best deal on a new computer.

He looked up and grinned. "Good morning to you."

She came up behind him, touching his shoulder, only as a show for the family, of course. Not because it felt so natural, so right. "Thank you for trying to help. I already told him it's impossi–"

"I fixed it."

Wait, what? "That's impossible. It's not repairable."

"Sure, it is." He stepped back, revealing the screen. "I didn't even have to reformat it. The data is still there."

"That can't be right." Adrianna sat in the chair next to him, rolling closer to the laptop. She tapped the rickety keyboard. "I spent six hours on this last week."

"As you can see, it's fine. In fact–" He winked. "I even improved it."

She should stay silent. Should hide the frustration that he fixed what she could not. Yet nerves were shattered, and her mouth decided to run away while leaving her brain behind. "Can it do the laundry?"

His lips curved up in a low, steady smile. "Why, of course."

"Well, I bet it can't fold clothing."

"It sure can." He winked. "It even puts them in the right drawers."

"Now you're just trying to impress me."

"Is it working?"

Yes.

Not because he'd created the first clothes-washing, laundry-folding computer, but because he'd fixed the unfixable, and hadn't deleted a file in the process. She'd asked colleagues and friends, had even emailed her college professor, about the issue. All of them agreed the computer was now a large paperweight. How could a man this gifted be a mere temp?

Or was he something else entirely?

"Wow." She turned away from his all-too-knowing gaze, settled on the neat row of laptops. Tried to focus. "I better get started on those, then."

"Actually, that's unnecessary. They're already done." He relaxed back in the chair. "I fixed them this morning."

How was it possible?

"Isn't he wonderful?" her mother gushed.

"A big help," her father added.

"A real keeper," Aunt Mabel announced.

Yes, he was. Only she couldn't keep him. This was a fake date, a fantasy. They didn't actually know each other, or at least she didn't know him. He'd seen a lot of her life, and thanks to a certain string bikini, of her. "How did you fix everything so fast?"

He shrugged. "I got up early."

"A week ago?"

He grinned and shook his head, as her mother moved forward. "Just be grateful. Now you have more time to swim." Her mother smiled at Nick, yet it wavered, and slowly faded. She squinted. "You know, you remind me of someone."

Nick's smile froze. What was wrong with him? By his expression, you'd think her mother offered him another dozen matzo balls. Of course, this was not the first time someone thought they recognized him.

"He's been told that before. By the po–" She clamped her mouth shut. Her mother would be mortified if she knew they'd been confronted by the law. Of course, when she found out why, she'd break out the "good" wine. "By a man at the rest stop," she finished quickly.

"Come to think of it, I thought you looked a little familiar, too," her father said. "Are you related to the Liebermans?"

Nick swiftly shook his head.

"The Kaplans?" her mother guessed.

"The Franks?" Aunt Mabel offered.

"The Rosenbergs?" Uncle Nathan hazarded.

He grinned, yet it was strained. "I'm afraid not. I just have one of those faces. People recognize me all the time." He wasn't lying, yet the explanation revealed nothing.

The mystery that was Nick Walters deepened.

⁂

"Mr. Dobbs is an excellent employee."

"Does Knight Technology have two men named Dobbs?"

Dominick tightened his fingers, loosened them when the delicate phone began to crack. How could Carlyle think Dobbs was competent, when he'd created a hostile work environment to rival a prison? Yet the problem was not limited to the Ft. Lauderdale office. Something far more devious lurked.

And Carlyle knew more than he was letting on.

He was going to find out what, in the few minutes he had before dinner. It had been an enjoyable day, too enjoyable, if such a thing were possible. They had visited a park, enjoying a picnic, biking and even a ride on a paddleboat. He'd enjoyed spending time with Adrianna to an extent he wouldn't explore, as well as her family. Lunch had been grand, and now they were relaxing after their showers.

"Don't worry." Carlyle regained his attention, his voice turning soothing. "Employees take advantage of employers all the time."

Unease intensified to outright suspicion, yet he would show none of it, at least not yet. "You are most likely correct."

"Of course, I am," Carlyle purred. "Why don't you take that European tour we discussed? I've taken the liberty of reserving your tickets for next month."

A hundred alarms blared a hundred warnings. This was

not the first time Carlyle overstepped his role. Yet Dominick kept his voice neutral. "I haven't decided on my schedule yet."

"Of course." The words held an unmistakable edge, curt, clipped and just on the wrong side of rude. Before he could respond, the phone clicked dead.

His suspicions increased a thousandfold.

"How did you do it?"

Dominick shot up his head. Adrianna was standing in the doorway, her lips a tight slash, her eyebrows knitted together. When had she arrived, and more importantly, what had she heard? He forced himself to remain calm as she padded into the room, her sneakers silent on the thick carpeting. "Do what?" The words emerged low, husky and *guilty*.

She stared, as responses flashed:
How did he fool everyone?
How did he deceive them?
How did he think he would get away with it?

Her gaze never wavered. "Fix the computer. You may pretend it was nothing, yet it was extraordinary."

Relief flared. She must not have heard him. "It's no big deal. I spend a lot of time troubleshooting IT problems."

She slowly encircled him. "I asked half a dozen people about that laptop, including a college professor. Everyone thought it was hopeless. Yet you managed to repair it in under an hour." She eyed him as if trying to discern some sort of puzzle. "I should ask for your autograph."

He choked out a laugh. What would she say if she knew he signed autographs regularly? "I was lucky enough to stumble onto the answer."

"Fixing six broken computers has nothing to do with luck."

No, it didn't. They were the same skills that allowed him to build a company worth billions, forging the cutting edge of computer science. The same attributes that made him a global leader in the field. And if he didn't do something, she was going to figure that out right here in her brother's childhood room. "You're right."

She halted. "I am?"

"I have a secret."

Her smile faded, replaced by sobriety, curiosity and *suspicion*. "Yes?"

"The truth is…" He breathed deeply. "I am actually the owner of… a magic wand."

"Oh you!" She reached out, tapped his chest. He grasped her hand, and suddenly all thoughts of circuits and chips and hard drives dissipated. It should have been cool in the air-conditioned room, yet it felt as hot as a South Florida scorcher. She leaned in, her fingers splaying against his chest, as he brought her closer… and closer… and closer.

"Children, it's time for dinner!"

Adrianna exhaled, leaned back. And the world turned cold. "I hope you don't mind her calling us children."

"Not at all." He *did* mind being interrupted before a kiss, but there was nothing to be done. He grasped her hand, not because it was time to play a part, and not even because he wanted to distract her, but because he simply wanted to. Hand-in-hand they walked to the living room, where everyone was gathered around an ornate table set with a veritable feast and topped with tall candles on pillars.

Mrs. Lewis handed them each a blue candle. "Usually Adrianna lights the candles, but I thought you could do it together."

Adrianna licked her lower lip. "I don't mind if he does it alone."

"Not at all." Placing a hand on the small of her back, he led her to the table. "I like sharing."

She visibly tightened, as if just realizing she'd been

ensnared. Yet as he positioned her in front of him, she leaned back, melting into his arms, where she belonged. Together, they lit the candles. As the flames flared, their bright orange fire representing so much, something else flared between the two of them.

Something he never wanted to end.

CHAPTER 7

The next few days brought enough emotions to fill her parents' swimming pool.

Happiness, enjoyment and satisfaction in the moments with Nick.

Concern, worry and anxiety as her family came closer to the truth.

And just about every emotion in between.

When her mother suggested they play a game several days later, Adrianna heartily agreed. Unlike swimming, there would be enough clothes to keep her from staring and enough people to stop the kisses she couldn't resist. No longer could she pretend it had anything to do with "practice." Everyone already believed they were a couple.

She was starting to believe it herself.

With every day, they grew closer, and it became harder to pretend the "pretend" was pretend. Nick was so kind, so friendly, so smart, everything she had on her boyfriend wish list. She loved her time with him, even as it came to an inevitable end.

He would be leaving soon.

Of course, there was still the matter of secrets. She kept gently prodding, yet somehow he always managed to change the subject, often with a kiss. She'd even gone so far as to Google his name, to ensure he wasn't actually a criminal, yet she found nothing.

It was almost as if Nick Walters didn't exist.

She couldn't press more at her parents' home, not when she had almost gotten away with the ruse. When they left, she would reveal her suspicions and ask for the truth.

Now she entered the living room with Nick by her side. His hand was around her waist, and they brushed against each other with every step. He pulled her a little closer.

"I have the perfect game." Her mother held up a blue box, emblazoned with the words "Couples Trivia." It showed a happy couple, with cards and questions that a couple *should* be able to answer. "Let's test how well you know each other."

Uh-oh. Adrianna slowed her steps. "I don't think that's a good idea."

"It'll be fun." Her mother pulled them to the sectional, where the rest of the family already sat. "Unless there's a reason you don't want to play."

"Of course not!" Adrianna cleared her throat, lowered her voice. "I mean, it sounds great."

"Perfect." Her mother grinned in victory. She got the game ready, as everyone partitioned into couples. "Nick can go first, since he's the guest." Nick rubbed his hands together, as if preparing for an Olympic race. Everyone leaned forward, as her mother opened the box and removed a crisp heart-shaped card. "First question: What is Adrianna's favorite meal?"

This was bad. Very, very bad. With all the meals they'd enjoyed together, had she actually told him she was a vegetarian? Her family served meat substitutes often, and he may not have realized he wasn't eating real meat.

Nick stroked his chin. "That's a hard one. She likes so many different things."

"That's right," she jumped in. "I really don't have a favorite."

"That's not true." Her mother patted her knee. "You've loved the same dish since you were three. You have it every year on your birthday."

"You just gave it away." Her father grasped her mother's hand, but his eyes were smiling. "Her birthday passed last month. Surely he remembers."

Nick squinted his eyes. "You like... chili."

Adrianna relaxed. Not because it was her favorite food – that would be pizza – but because it was a reasonable answer. Of course, her parents would assume he meant veggie chili. Her mother frowned, yet didn't jump up and immediately accuse her of recruiting a fake date for the occasion.

"She especially likes the meat."

Well, there it was.

"The ground beef is just delicious," he continued his one-man sabotage, "She's a big fan." He stopped, clearly noticing the scrutiny and silence. He chuckled nervously. "Don't worry – the meat was organic."

Could this get any worse?

"Of course it was organic." She grasped his hand. "After all, it was *veggie* meat."

He blinked.

She blinked.

The entire family blinked.

"Obviously, it was veggie meat." He gave a desperate laugh. "Because she is a vegetarian."

"Of course." Everyone laughed, except her mother, who was gazing at Nick as if trying to decipher whether he was joking or truly hadn't known. She plucked the card out of her mother's hand and placed it back in the box. "Whose turn is it now?"

"Yours, of course."

Of course.

She reached into the box and removed an innocuous-appearing red heart. She twisted the thick card in her hand and read, "What's your favorite color?"

Thank goodness. She could make up any color, and he would agree. She opened her mouth, just as her mother spoke, "That's too easy. Even I know the answer to that."

Adrianna gaped. "You do?"

"Of course, my dear." Her mother tapped her arm. "Remember, we had a whole conversation about it?"

They had? She closed her eyes, as she tried to remember the many conversations they had about her supposed boyfriend. It was there, at the back of her mind. She shot up. "It's pink! He loves the color pink!"

Silence.

Her mother wore a genuine smile this time, while assorted family members sported unabashed amusement. And Nick? He was opening and closing his mouth like a bobbing fish.

"Don't be ashamed, honey. I'm sure plenty of men would choose pink as their favorite color."

He folded his arms across his chest.

"Not just any pink," her mom chimed in helpfully. "Bubblegum pink."

His gaze darkened.

"Well, then." She smiled. "Who's next?"

※

"You told them my favorite color was bubblegum pink?"

From across the cozy corner loveseat, Adrianna cringed,

before glancing around the living room to make certain no one had overheard. The game had finished, amazingly without them being outed as "Fake Couple of the Year," and the others were now preparing dinner. It had been close, however, and they earned more than their share of curious glances.

Now she whispered, "My mother was concerned by all the rugged activities I gave you. I had to make you appear softer."

He folded his arms across his chest. "You don't think I'm soft?"

"Actually, I'd say you're quite hard." She flushed, licked her lower lip, and he resisted the urge to trace his finger across it. To lean forward and taste. Simply to hold her.

She inspired a lot of urges, many far deeper than physical. The strong, smart woman attracted him like no one ever before, with her fascinating conversation, clever wit and uncompromising generosity. His feelings for her were anything but pretend.

How could he give her up?

A relationship would be a challenge. She didn't even know his real name. Yet no matter how many times he listed the obstacles, his determination never wavered. He wanted more.

But first he had to tell her the truth.

"You didn't know I was a vegetarian."

He grimaced. "I thought I saw you eat meat. You should have mentioned it when we were discussing our habits."

"You're right." She frowned. "Next time I have a fake boyfriend, it will be the first thing I share."

No.

She would not have another fake boyfriend. Not another boyfriend at all.

"Look at all this." Mrs. Lewis strode into the room, flipping through the mail like a Fortune 500 CEO. She held up a magazine and frowned. "I can't believe your brother forwards his mail every time he comes here on vacation."

Adrianna looked upward and smiled. Nick returned it, just as her mother stacked the letters. He froze at the image glaring from the back of a magazine:

Him.

He barely remembered the magazine shoot, which was part of a campaign for one of his charities and featured a close headshot. Even with the cleanshaven face and different haircut, he was clearly identifiable. If they saw it, the ruse would be over – for good.

"Adrianna, can you put these in the den? Joshua's mail is on the coffee table."

"Of course." Adrianna reached for the stack, her fingers wrapping around the neck of his printed picture.

He jumped up. "Let me help you with that."

Adrianna looked up in surprise. "You don't have to–"

He grabbed it out of her hands. She stared, yet he hadn't a choice. If she saw his picture, it would be the blue screen of death. "I'm just trying to be a courteous guest." And as any courteous guest would do, he turned and fled.

"Wait up."

He moved quicker.

He reached the den just before she jogged up to him. Unable to discard all manners, he gestured for her to go ahead, then walked straight to the coffee table and slammed down the mail. Suspicion and curiosity tangled in her emerald gaze, as she looked from the mail to him and then back again. She sifted through the letters, grasped the magazine.

His picture was not on the cover. However, the front page did contain–

"Dominick Knight."

He tightened. "I'm sorry?"

"You must be familiar with the CEO of Knight Technology." She pointed at the name in two-inch letters. "Famous, rich and powerful."

How did he respond to that? "I do know him. Well. Really well. Extremely well."

That didn't sound suspicious or anything.

She looked at him strangely. "He's incredible. Built the entire company with hard work, determination and a genius IQ. He's the reason I applied for the job in the first place."

Wow. "Really?"

She nodded. "It's also why I'm so disappointed with the horrible conditions. I wonder if he has any idea of what it's become."

He hadn't. It was no excuse. "He should know," he said softly.

"I suppose you're right," she murmured. "Still, I'd like to believe he's a good guy, who employs some not so good guys."

Still no excuse. "Hopefully, he will realize it."

She nodded, tracing her fingers over the letters of his name. "He wrote a book about computers, life and all sorts of things. It motivated a lot of people, including my brother and me." She tossed the magazine down on the table. "I admire Knight, but Joshua idolizes him. He knows his entire life history."

A buzzing sounded in his ears. If her brother knew him that well, he could very well recognize him.

How would he hack his way out of this one?

CHAPTER 8

It was time to reveal the truth.

Exposure was inevitable, and ever-closer, with Joshua's arrival the next evening, the day of the anniversary party and their last day here. If Adrianna discovered the truth at the same time as her family, disaster would ensue, and the entire ploy would be compromised. If it somehow made its way to the media, it would cause true disaster. Yet despite all these reasons, one thing mattered more.

Dominick couldn't bear to keep the secret from Adrianna any longer.

What started as an innocent ruse had turned into something more deceptive, more duplicitous. He'd justified it with his altruistic aim, yet somewhere along the way, motivations and consequences transformed, and misdirection turned into outright dishonesty.

He hated lying to her.

Something had shifted these past days. His world, his goals, *him*. Emotions surged, faster and further reaching than any in his life. Spending time with Adrianna recaptured good times of the past, when he was just a kid with a computer and a dream. Somehow he'd become the man in the ivory tower, the person sitting behind a desk and a hundred assistants, managing people, or as he was beginning to suspect, being managed himself. Here he was part of something, helping her family, enjoying life, not simply watching it. She brought back the past, redefined the present.

She was his future.

For a man who dabbled in zeros and ones, emotions were not easy. Yet sometimes the heart just knows.

Wait. It almost sounded like he–

"Don't you just love it?"

Yes, he did.

"I do."

Adrianna smiled. Yet she did not know the question she had truly asked, the answer he gave. How could he have missed it? Perhaps because he'd never felt this way before, and yet now it was so clear. He now knew how he felt about this woman. Not because of what they shared, but because of the emotions it revealed. He was meant to care for this woman, hold her, keep her safe and happy.

He loved this woman.

They had not known each other long, yet his soul recognized hers.

A deep breath in, a deep breath out. "Adrianna, I have something to tell–"

"Nick, I want to tell you–"

They chuckled, as much in unison as their words. "Go ahead," he said softly. Their days may be dreadfully short, yet tonight the hours were endless. "What do you want to tell me?"

"Actually, I want to *show* you something." She reached for him. "Come with me?" He grasped her hand, and the familiar connection sparked.

Then he followed the woman he loved into the darkness.

❧

It shouldn't matter that his eyes lit up whenever they touched.

That he looked at her like she was the most precious treasure in the world.

That his smile made everything perfect.

Yet as they sat under endless stars in a velvet sky, somehow it all mattered.

"This is breathtaking."

"Yes, it is." Blue waters sparkled like diamonds under the brilliant moonlight, their lapping waves accompanying the nightbirds' melody. Lilies scented the cool night air, from the luscious blooms that grew along the bank of the large lake. It was lovely and it was enchanting, most of all because of the man sitting next to her. "I can't think of anything more beautiful."

"I can." He gazed at her.

She blushed across her entire body.

He scooted just a little closer to her on the pier, brushing against her side and eliciting streaks of sensation. The night was perfection defined, and so was the man. She never wanted to leave.

His gaze wandered to the cozy cottage behind them. Emerald vines sprinkled with violet flowers covered whitewashed walls, with matching wildflowers overflowing from flower boxes in large picture windows. "Is that where Joshua will stay?"

She nodded. "I'll show you the cottage a little later, if you'd like."

He nodded and relaxed back, yet a furrow appeared in his brow. Was he finally going to share his secret? She held her breath, waiting as he took his own. He opened his mouth…

"Tell me about your brother."

Clearly, that was not the elucidation he wanted to share. She bit back a thousand questions. "Like me, Joshua loves computers. It's ironic since our parents have no background in technology." She smiled softly. "It didn't matter. They were happy with everything we did. No matter our interests, they always supported us. It's what inspired me to pursue my own business."

She pursed her lips. She hadn't meant to reveal that, yet the expected discomfort was absent. "I'd ask you not to share that, but I don't think it's necessary. For some reason, I trust you."

Something flashed in his eyes. "Adrianna, I– I–" He halted. "I think it's great your parents were so supportive. Mine weren't at first," he admitted. "My entire family is in the medical field. Both my parents are doctors, and they assumed I would also be a doctor."

"Dr. Nick." She smiled. "Did you ever consider it?"

"I did, but there was one problem."

"What's that?"

"I get positively nauseous every time I see a drop of blood."

She laughed. "That's a pretty big obstacle for a physician."

"It wouldn't have mattered. Computers have been my passion ever since I was a little kid. My parents became more supportive when I did well."

She hid her frown. He worked for a cutting-edge company, yet only as a temporary employee. It seemed unlikely to delight demanding parents. Of course, with his skills, he should be running the company. She frowned…

"Have you ever considered working with Joshua?" His question snagged her attention. "Perhaps forming a company together?"

She shook her head. "I considered it, but logistically it

would be too difficult. He doesn't live close enough to me. Plus, he likes working in big companies."

"So you are considering a partner?"

A negative danced on her tongue, yet the word wouldn't form. It was strange, since she hadn't considered anyone except Joshua. Yet maybe...

Was she seriously considering asking a man she'd only known for weeks to join her business venture? It was far riskier than pretending he was her fake date. That had an ending date, but any partnership would be continuous. Of course, it meant something else could continue.

Them.

Yet before she even considered working together, she had to discover the secrets he hid. "You said you had something to tell me."

He visibly tightened, then nodded ever-so-perceptibly. "Adrianna, I–"

Laughter chimed from a group in the distance, snagging their attention. As a group of teens walked on the far side of the lake, Nick exhaled. "Why don't you show me the cottage? We can talk there."

Was the secret so great, others couldn't hear? She showed none of her concern as she allowed him to lead her to the building. The laughter faded as they entered a cozy space scented with apple and cinnamon. The cottage shrunk with the massive man's presence, yet it remained charming. Paintings of Florida sunsets covered cream-colored walls, bordered by azure trim. Two large, checked sofas made for a quaint seating area, while a small cherry wood table took up a side, flanked by natural wood chairs.

Nick traced his hand along the mantle of a rare Florida fireplace, gazing at the small glass sculptures of sea creatures adorning it. "This is fantastic."

"Thank you." She picked up a picture frame with glued on

seashells. It had been her anniversary gift to her parents when she was eight. "I used to sneak in here whenever I needed privacy. Although I just had one brother, family was always visiting." She held out her hand. "Don't get me wrong. I loved seeing them."

"Just sometimes a kid needs a little quiet."

He understood. "Now I wish I could go back and spend more time with them. Does that seem funny?"

He smiled warmly. "Not at all. It just means you have the right priorities."

So did he. He spoke of his family often, and helped hers incessantly, showing his kindness. He wandered slowly around the room, stopping at the small love seat. "Why don't you sit down?"

That was ominous. She trudged forward, sinking down on a sofa that smelled like her mother's perfume. He sat next to her, causing her stomach to flutter like the waves of the seascape above the mantle. "Is everything all right?"

He ducked his head, and a lock of dark hair fell over his eyes. She resisted the urge to smooth it back. "What's wrong?"

His smile was clearly strained, liquid eyes holding nameless secrets. She followed his gaze to the picture of her brother. *Of course.* "You don't need to be nervous." Relief softened every muscle. "I know what this is about."

His eyes widened. "You do?"

"Of course." She gave in to her urge and pushed aside his hair before touching his shoulder. "It's because of Joshua, isn't it?"

Under her hand, muscles tightened. And at this completely inappropriate, utterly inopportune time, something else flared:

Desire.

It wasn't fair. He was just so handsome. And muscular.

And still really, really handsome. And if she didn't get herself under control she was going to do something that would make every part of her blush... again. She cleared her throat. "Didn't you think I would figure it out?"

He opened his mouth. "I... I wasn't sure."

"Well, of course, I did." She let go of his shoulder. "It's pretty obvious."

He clasped her hands. "You're not mad?"

"Not even a little. Now that we've established you're uncomfortable meeting a big brother while pretending to date his little sister, I have something to tell you."

He looked stricken. "No, Adrianna, I–

"I've developed feelings for you."

She'd shocked him into silence. Well, shock and unmistakable male satisfaction. "Feelings?"

Why did it suddenly feel like she was back in second grade, asking Bobby Mendelson if he wanted to share her fruit snacks? "Yes, feelings." Heat turned her blood to a low boil. "Good ones."

His lips curved upwards. The heat notched up several thousand degrees. "I was wondering–" She started an intense study of her cuticles. "If you have any..." She moved to the other hand. "What I mean to say is do you..."

"Have feelings?" He edged closer. "Have you noticed how much practice we've shared?"

Forget turning on the fireplace. She *was* the fireplace. "I wasn't sure if that was for the family."

He reached out and grasped her cheek. She leaned into it. "Adrianna, we practiced three hundred and forty-two times."

"I'm not sure that number is accurate." She bit her lip. "But I'm willing to attempt it."

His eyes darkened. "It really is important to practice."

"They say practice makes perfect."

Then, they *practiced*.

He was strength, heat, desire and pure passion. He immediately took control of the kiss, wrapping his arms around her as he brought her close for his administrations. His lips were firm and pliant, as he caressed, tasted and tested. She opened her mouth to give him better access, pressing closer, still it wasn't close enough.

Suddenly, the urge to do more – much more – surged. She pushed forward, splaying her hands on his chest. The muscles jumped under her, as she pressed flush against him. Her breasts brushed against his chest, as heaviness permeated her body, streaking desire in sensitive spots. She was raw need, pure unadulterated sensation.

"You're so beautiful," He trailed kisses down her neck. "Breathtaking."

"Would you like to see more?"

He stilled. Had she mistaken his intentions? The passion burning in his eyes said no. "I can't tell you how much I want this, but I don't want to take advantage of you."

"You're not taking advantage of me." She smoothed his flat stomach. Heat burned through the thin shirt. "I want this."

He stared for a moment more. "I want this, too, but it can't be about the ruse." He held her gaze. "This is no longer pretend."

No, it wasn't. Something altogether wonderful leapt within her. "I didn't know if you felt it, too," she whispered.

"To an extent words cannot describe."

He leaned down, pressing his lips to hers. The future was unwritten and unspoken, yet by her feelings, and the hint in his eyes, just perhaps they could forge something amazing. They moved unhurriedly now, as they explored each other. She closed her eyes as he grasped the hem of her dress and lifted it over her head. Always one to be fair, she unbuttoned his shirt, slowly revealing the abs that had been flashing in her mind ever since their swim. It was like unwrapping all your birthday presents at once, as he shrugged off the shirt. She pressed into him with lace-covered breasts, yet it still wasn't enough.

He understood every question she couldn't ask. He reached behind her, and suddenly the binding around her breasts loosened. They were heavy and achy as he lifted the bra away, exposing her to his perusal. Then he *worshipped* them. Her breaths came in a series of gasps as he traced, cupped, weighed and molded. She clutched his hair as he kissed each straining peak. "Closer," she gasped.

Sapphire eyes sparkled. "As you wish."

He took but a moment to divest himself of the rest of his clothing. Her breath caught at his sheer magnificence. "You were hiding," she accused.

His smoldering gaze pinned her, then he traced his finger along the seam of her most feminine place. "Now let's see what you're hiding." He slipped a finger into the scrap of lace, slowly bringing it down. He stood back and *studied* her. "You are..." His voice trailed off, but dilated eyes revealed all. "Stunning."

The heat turned into an inferno.

He was predator, she was prey and he *devoured* her. He explored with his lips, with his hands, everything and everywhere open to his administrations. She gasped as he captured her in his arms. "What are you doing?" she breathed, as he lifted her naked body. Bare skin to bare skin, hard to soft, claiming to yielding.

"Taking you to bed," he rumbled, as he strode through the cottage to the master bed. He swept aside the silky bedspread, splaying her on the buttery sheets. She'd never been so exposed, so open. "Beautiful."

Her response was lost in the kiss.

Suddenly he was everywhere, surrounding her,

enveloping her, *possessing* her. Thoughts scattered as he explored, deepening the kisses, setting her entire body afire as he caressed, petted and fondled. She pulled him closer, telling him without words she was ready, yet he forced her to wait in blissful agony, bringing her to the edge for an eternity and more. Finally, when she thought she could take no more, they became one.

She moaned as he filled her to utter perfection. He was so much larger than she, yet they fit together perfectly, as if forged for each other. The crescendo grew higher, higher, higher, as he brought her to heights of which she never dreamed. Just when she could take no more…

She shattered.

Early morning light streamed through wide windows, their radiant beams lighting the cottage in amber brilliance. Dominick opened his eyes, stretching on the luxurious bed. He'd never been so content, so satisfied, and not because of the plush mattress, the pleasant morning coolness or the sweet sounds of the birds chirping outside, but because of the beautiful woman curled beside him.

Making love to her had been like nothing before. She was beauty defined, enchanting, passionate, responsive. Yet it was not the physical connection that made their joining so spectacular. It was something far deeper, something elemental, instinctual.

It was as if his heart recognized hers.

"Hi."

He softened at the light voice, as she blinked up at him, unfocused eyes straddling the border between reality and dreams.

"Hi you," he murmured. "Did you have a good night's sleep?"

"It's morning?" She gasped.

"It's morning." He smiled.

"It's morning." She cringed.

"It's morning." He frowned.

She sprung out of bed and plucked her dress off the bed. "This can't be happening." She grasped her bra off the floor. "We didn't actually do this." She took assorted clothing off the lamp, television and ceiling fan. It really had been an enjoyable night. "How did I allow this to happen?"

He scooted forward, grasping his clothing. He slid on his pants. "I've never been so flattered in all my life."

She stopped, clutching the clothing in her hands. Her lips parted into a little O. "I didn't mean– I wasn't talking about–"

"It's okay." He lifted himself off the bed, and slowly approached her. He grasped her hands. "Just breathe. Everything will be all right."

She inhaled deeply, and her color deepened from winter white to a soft blush. "I wasn't talking about what we did. That was…" She bit her luscious lower lip, and his eyes tracked down. It was all he could do not to nip it.

Soon.

"It was extraordinary," she breathed. "But I never meant to stay out the entire night. My family…"

He winced, and he was again a teenage boy, bringing back a date ten minutes (or hours) beyond curfew. "Any chance they didn't realize we were missing?"

She grimaced. "My mother noticed when we arrived three minutes late for dinner."

True. She'd also seemed particularly interested as to why they'd been late (they had been kissing). Of course they didn't tell her (they had been kissing). However, her smile made clear she knew (they had been kissing).

If that was how she reacted when they were three minutes late, it did not bode well for six hundred minutes late. He pulled on his shirt, shoes and socks as she donned the rest of her clothing, then took a precious few minutes to change the sheets and straighten the cottage. "Let's go." He took a step, stopped. "Wait." They couldn't leave yet. He hadn't told her the truth – not about who he was, and not about how he felt.

Not about the future he saw in her eyes.

Tonight her brother would arrive, and his cover would almost certainly be destroyed. If he didn't tell her before then, he could lose everything. Yet even as he reached her, she strode forward, her dark hair swishing in the morning breeze. "We have to get back. We can talk at the house."

He set his jaw, yet said nothing as they strode side by side. Yet just as they reached the door, it opened from the inside. Mrs. Lewis appeared in the doorway, wearing a bright blue sweater and a beaming smile. "Glad to see you two finally made it back."

Well, this was awkward. Dominick couldn't stop a grimace, yet it froze as a tall man emerged behind Mrs. Lewis. With the same dark hair and green eyes as Adrianna, there was no mistaking the handsome man.

The man smiled, but it faded as he turned to him. Confusion flared, then surprise and finally astonishment. Then two whispered words changed everything.

"Dominick Knight?"

CHAPTER 9

Reality shattered.

It rearranged, reformed, emerging as something entirely different. It couldn't be.

"You look different with the beard, but it's you, right?" Joshua strode to the man beside her. "I would recognize you anywhere."

Deny it. Tell him it's not true. Nick Walters cannot be Dominick Knight.

Yet instead, the man next to her said quietly, "I am Dominick Knight."

Someone gasped. Several someones, actually, and in the back of her mind, she realized one was her. "No," she breathed. He reached for her, but she backed up. "You can't be Dominick Knight. You're Nick Walters, the temp who–"

"No." The single word, so strongly spoken, so different than Nick's gentle cadence. She closed her eyes.

Nick Walters didn't exist.

"I wanted to tell you–"

"No," Now she stopped him, as every muscle clenched. "You're the famous Dominick Knight, billionaire owner of

83

Knight Technology, bestselling author, international celebrity."

"Adrianna–"

"Was this some sort of game?" She backed up, out of his reach. "How could you lie to me?"

He took another step. "If you'd let me explain–"

"No." She held up a hand. "I don't want you to explain. I thought–" She sucked in a breath of his heady scent. "It doesn't matter what I thought. I cared about a man who isn't real. Nick Walters doesn't exist."

"That's not true." His voice deepened. "My name may be different, but I'm the same person."

"No, you're not," she hissed. "You were a regular guy, a temporary employee with exemplary computer skills. Yet instead, you're a billionaire computer genius who runs an international juggernaut. Was this some sort of joke? A prank? Can you imagine how it feels to be deceived by someone you care about?"

She froze.

"Oh my goodness," she whispered. "I did the exact same thing." She turned from the man she thought she cared about – no, the man she *did* care about. Despite the revelations, her feelings had not changed. Yet now she had her own secrets to reveal. "I've been lying to you."

Eyes blinked and lips parted, and a sea of guilt swept through her. Her mother stepped forward. "You said you didn't know."

"I didn't know about Mr. Knight. Like you, I believed he was Nick Walters. But he isn't–" Her voice broke. "He isn't my boyfriend. I made it all up."

Her mother's face turned as white as the wedding dress she'd undoubtedly imagined for her and Nick's wedding. "I don't understand."

"I thought I was doing the right thing, by not ruining

your anniversary. Now I realize how very wrong it was." Dominick looked so forlorn, it took every bit of strength not to throw herself into his arms, tell him she didn't care about lies, misdirection or secret identities. Yet she had to stay strong. If he lied about who he was, what else he lied about? His thoughts? His motives?

His feelings?

"You should leave."

The words came as if from someone else. She didn't want him to leave, not really, and that was why it was so important he did. The thought of being separated slayed her, but at least for now, she needed time – and space – to sort through the new reality.

Dominick stood as straight as a two by four. "Adrianna, please–" Yet she turned away, as his expression turned to stone. Seconds and an eternity passed. "I will go, for now."

"I'm so sorry," she whispered to her mother, to her family, to the heart shattered in a million pieces. Dominick reached for her once more, but she backed up. If only she could shut her heart to the man who still had the power to move her. "I need time… please."

She couldn't look at him. If she did, she would beg him to stay, tell him the past didn't matter. "I'm so sorry," she whispered once more. Then she fled from the man she desired, the family she deceived, the future that could never be hers.

Shattered.

⁂

"I CAN'T BELIEVE IT." Joshua turned the wheel of the large minivan, taking a sharp turn down the two-lane street. "Adrianna has never done anything like that before. What was she thinking?"

Another mile further from the woman he adored.

MELANIE KNIGHT

Dominick gazed out the window, at a sunny day completely opposite to the storm raging inside. The trees passed by in an emerald sea, each taking him away from his path, both literally and figuratively, and closer to an airport that would take him ever further. "She did it for your parents." He inhaled. "I'm not saying it was right, but it was not about embarrassment or deception. She didn't want to ruin an occasion that meant so much to her family."

Joshua stayed still for a moment, before slowly responding, "Adrianna always thinks of others before herself. She's the first person to share, the first to offer assistance, the first to brighten someone's day."

She had not brightened his day. She had brightened his life.

Another mile further from the woman he cherished.

"What about you?"

Dominick looked up sharply. "What about me?"

"Why did you do it?" Unlike Adrianna, his voice held no accusation, but instead curiosity, compassion. "I'm sure Adrianna told you how much I idolize you. I've read your book three times, and I've seen your lectures twice that. I can't imagine you did this as some sort of prank. You must have a good reason."

Dominick tightened. "I do." His campaign for his business was as much a disaster as the scheme he'd concocted with Adrianna. Clearly, his organization possessed a massive problem, which had been progressing steadily before he even noticed. If only Carlyle hadn't repeatedly reassured him all was well…

He froze. With all the problems, why hadn't Carlyle noticed?

Change of plans. "Can you take me to the local Knight Technology office instead of the airport?" He couldn't give up the woman he loved. Yet to win his case, he would have to do something massive.

The next moments blurred together, until Joshua pulled into the large, rounded driveway of Knight Technology's sleek five-story Orlando office. Dominick grabbed his bag and disembarked, but before he could shut the door, Joshua leaned forward. "Do want me to pick you up?"

At any other time, Dominick would have smiled. He'd deceived his family, yet still the man was willing to give him the benefit of the doubt and help him. Apparently, kindness ran in the family. He could use a man like that in the company.

If matters progressed as he believed, there would be an opening in upper management soon.

✦

"You want to forgive him, don't you?"

The sun-splashed lake sparkled like a sea of diamonds, its edges framed by colorful lilies, their brilliant violet, white and yellow blooms casting a rainbow on Earth. The air was cool and fresh, scented by the flowers and a million memories. It had been the glistening backdrop to their one magical night.

Adrianna never hated the word *one* so much.

"Would it be so wrong if I forgave him?" She shielded her eyes against the sun, watched the silvery fish threading playfully around green turtles. "He deceived me."

Her mother sank down on the pier next to her, dangling her legs over the edge. "You deceived us, too." The words were soft, yet they pierced an already acidic stomach.

"I'm so sorry about that," Adrianna whispered.

Her mother rubbed her back. "It's all right, sweetheart. I was angry at first, and hurt, but I understand why you did it.

You were trying to protect us, but we'd rather you be honest." Her mother pulled her into a hug. "I'm also partly to blame."

"What?" Adrianna sat up. "That isn't even a little true."

"Isn't it?" Her mother raised an eyebrow. "It didn't bother you that I asked about a boyfriend fifteen times every conversation?"

"It wasn't fifteen." Despite the tumultuous situation, Adrianna couldn't stop a small smile. "It couldn't have been more than fourteen."

"Exactly." Her mother chuckled. "The point is, I shouldn't have been so nosy, or made you feel like there was something wrong if you didn't have a boyfriend. You are absolutely wonderful, all on your own. I love you so much, Adrianna."

Her vision turned just a little blurrier, as her mother swept her into another hug. "I love you, too, Mom." The world seemed a little less bleak as her mother held her, surrounding her in unconditional love, as she always had. Yet far too soon, the present returned, and she let out a shuddering breath. "I just can't believe it was all pretend."

"Oh, there was nothing pretend about Nick's feelings."

She looked up sharply.

"There wasn't." Her mother reached into her purse and rifled through an entire convenience store before taking out a miniature box of tissues. She handed her three. "He may have lied about his name and position, but he didn't lie about his feelings. You can see it in his eyes. He's crazy about you."

Was it possible? She squeezed the tissues into a crumpled mass. "If that's true, why did he hide who he really was?"

"I don't know." Her mother rubbed her arm. "Perhaps there's more at stake than we realize. The only person who can explain is him."

Yet she'd sent him away without allowing a word, while her own family not only listened but understood. What had she done? "I have to let him explain." She swallowed. "How could I send away the man I lov–" She gasped.

And her mother beamed. "What is that, dear?"

"The man I love." The last word was a mere whisper on the wind, its meaning far eclipsing its breathless utterance. "Do I love a man who doesn't exist?"

"Not at all." Her mother softened. "What do you love about him?"

A thousand memories swirled, amidst a thousand answers. "I love his kindness and his generosity. He's so giving to everyone, even at his own expense. He's funny, charming and so brilliant. What he did with those computers was unbelievable, but at the same time, he's so modest about it. I love our conversations and the moments we spend with each other. I love… everything."

"Those are all wonderful things," her mother agreed. "And what you didn't say is as important as what you did."

Adrianna lifted her chin. "What didn't I say?"

Her mother counted on her fingers. "His name, job, bank account, popularity, fame."

"None of those things matter." The answer was automatic, and so very true. "I don't like being deceived, of course, yet it's no different than what I did."

"And he may have just as altruistic a reason," her mother pointed out.

"How could I let him go?" Her heart lurched. "I have to tell him how I feel." She pushed herself up. "Maybe he's still at the airport. This time of year, it may take a while to get a flight."

Her mother rose next to her. "There's only one way to find out."

Adrianna took a step towards the house, yet stopped as her brother slammed open the door.

"Come quick," he yelled. "You're going to want to see this."

※

ONCE AGAIN, he was Dominick Knight.

The beard was gone, and so was the bad haircut. The ill-fitting clothing was in the donation bin, and his suit was back. As he stood at the podium, ready to address a dozen news stations, the world and the woman he loved, he was back to himself. But he was not the same.

These past weeks, he remembered who Dominick Knight was. He wasn't the pampered executive in the high-rise penthouse, but the man who loved to tinker in a room full of computers, working alongside others. He was the man who enjoyed a boisterous family, homemade meals and a simple evening by a lake. But most of all, he was the man who fell in love with the most amazing woman, a kind and spirited beauty he already missed. A woman for whom he would fight.

In a few hours, he realized the extent of the corruption infiltrating his business. Carlyle had been the mastermind, poised at the helm as he hired "business associates" with little ability to manage but copious amounts of *creativity* when it came to accounting. Dominick's team had found numerous discrepancies and already turned them in to the authorities.

Matters would be made right. Employees would be compensated, and workplaces made *superb*. All involved parties had already been fired, with civic *and* criminal investigators perusing enough evidence to keep them busy for a year. He would spend as long as it took to make it right.

Yet right now, there was something else he had to fix.

His future depended on it.

CHAPTER 10

"Is that Nick?" Aunt Mabel exclaimed.

"It can't be," her uncle replied.

"That's definitely Nick," her mother responded.

"No," Adrianna breathed. "That's *Dominick*."

She barely recognized the man who stood alone at the podium. Instead of baggy clothing, he wore an Armani business suit, cut to luxurious precision. Instead of soft waves, his hair was flawless in a stiff thousand-dollar haircut. He was freshly shaven, chiseled features sculpted and defined.

Her father was clearly astonished. "How is he on television?"

"He's the billionaire owner of one of the largest companies in the world," Joshua responded. "When he calls an impromptu press conference, the news stations come running. Someone called and told us to turn on this channel, then hung up without identifying himself."

"What could he possibly have to say?"

Dominick answered the question. "Thank you for coming on such short notice." His voice boomed across the room, so similar and yet so different from Nick's. It held unmistakable power, the tone of a man accustomed to leading. "News of this will reach the business world tomorrow, and I want you to hear it from me first. These past weeks I went undercover at Knight Technology to investigate rumors of mismanagement. To my dismay, we found evidence of numerous wrongdoings, enough to call in the authorities. Be assured I will personally address any and all issues. As CEO, I take full responsibility, and I will not stop until everything is set right."

He paused. "My other news is far more personal. Some would say too personal to share, and yet I want the world to understand what is truly in my heart. While I was undercover, I met an extraordinary woman, a caring, smart and spirited beauty who enchanted me. I never believed love could come this quickly, yet no other word could describe it. I will forever regret my dishonesty, and hope she gives me another chance. I love you, Adrianna, and have a very important question to ask you."

Her breath hitched. He couldn't mean...

She blinked as the screen abruptly turned from Nick to a roundtable of suited business analysts. After a brief conversation where they pondered the identity of the "mystery woman," they focused on the business side of the announcement. Her family didn't say a word as the newscasters discussed it with experts from around the world. Apparently, the investigation had already started, and they praised Dominick for his quick response. After a few minutes, her unusually silent mother stood, and turned off the television.

Adrianna exhaled a shaky breath. "Did that really happen?"

"Yes, it did." Her mother's eyes sparkled. "How do you feel?"

She swallowed. "I– I–" The doorbell rang, cutting off the words. Her throat dried. "Are you expecting someone?"

Her mother shook her head. "You should get it." She touched her arm, guiding her forward. "I have a feeling it's for you."

Adrianna tensed, as the others urged her on with nods and smiles. One step in front of the other, then another and another until she stood at the front door. With a deep breath, she opened it.

It. Was. Him.

The man she knew well and not at all.

The man who made her smile and laugh.

The man she *loved*.

"How are you here?" she breathed.

He gave a soft smile, and a dimple appeared in his cheek, yet another feature his disguise had concealed. "I recorded it nearby and had a car ready. I wanted to be here as soon as possible." He clasped her fingers. "I'm so sorry, Adrianna. I never meant to deceive you for so long. I started to tell you a hundred times."

"Why didn't you?" Every emotion threatened to burst forth. "I would have understood, especially for such an important reason."

"I know you would have." He looked down. "I was afraid you wouldn't notice the man in Dominick Knight's shadow. People see the CEO, the author, the celebrity. I thought you'd look at me differently if you knew the truth."

She traced her finger along his smooth chin, lifting it to gaze into sapphire eyes. "I don't care if you're a temp or a billionaire, a celebrity or an ordinary man. Your resume is not what attracted me. You may have lied about your name, but you showed your real self. Were you truthful about your feelings for me?"

"Always." Honesty burned in his eyes. "Being with you is like finding a hidden treasure. You are everything I could ever want and more, like finding my missing piece, my heart's dream."

She blinked as the world started to blur. "I love you, too. I don't know how it happened so quickly, but–"

"When it's right–"

"You just know."

Locked in each other's eyes, the world sparkled. "I do have some advice. You should fire Dobbs."

He laughed, as he gazed at her with pure adoration. "I've done that and more. I'll make certain to replace him with a manager who respects and appreciates our employees. I'm actually going to need people for C level positions, in case a certain brother would be interested."

A gasp came from the adjoining room.

He grinned wider, but then it faded. "I would ask you, but I know you're planning to leave the company. Your skills are incredible, and you were mistreated to an appalling extent. You are welcome to stay in any capacity, but if you want to start your own business, I fully support you. I would love to invest... or be a partner."

"A partner sounds great." She beamed. "In all ways."

"I'm glad you feel that way, because I did mention a question." He removed a small blue box from his pocket. She brought her hands to her mouth, as he sank to one knee. He opened the box to reveal a stunning vintage ring, its center a massive round diamond, its edges a halo of smaller diamonds. It was a masterpiece of nature, artistry and *love*.

"Adrianna, I love you more than words can express. You are gorgeous inside and out, so kind and caring, brilliant and beautiful. I love the time we spend together, talking, jogging or having a splash fight, for every moment with you is delightful. You are my perfect piece of code, and my destiny." The words sparkled with love. "Will you marry me?"

There was only one answer she could ever give. "Yes," She grasped his hands, lifting him up. "Yes, yes, yes!"

He grinned so widely, she laughed. He slid the ring on her finger, where it fit to perfection. "Should we practice kissing?"

"Definitely."

She gasped in delight as he pressed those luscious lips to hers. Passion sparked from a kiss of true and perfect love. She could have stayed there forever, locked in the embrace of the man she loved, yet there would be time. After all, they had a lifetime to share. "Should we tell the family?"

He smiled, showing his dimples. "I don't think that will be necessary." He pointed behind her. Her entire extended family waved and cheered.

Strong arms came around her. She leaned back into warmth, security and most of all love. "I adore you," she whispered.

He placed a soft kiss on her head. "And I adore you."

"So–" Her mother beamed. "How many do you want?"

"How many matzo balls?" Nick winked.

Her mother gave the smile of all contented mothers. "Children?"

And instead of cringing, Adrianna and Nick only smiled wider.

EPILOGUE

"I can't believe you fooled everyone." Royce Livingston relaxed in the wingback chair, swirling the amber liquor in the cut crystal glass. The drink sparkled in the light from the massive marble fireplace, reflecting golden on the oversized mahogany furniture, plush sofas and priceless antiques. Scented with oak and the subtle fragrance of custom cologne, the chamber was opulence defined, underscored by classical music through a hidden speaker so crisp, it sounded as if they were in the pit.

It was typical luxury for the Billionaires of Miami, the moniker the press had dubbed their group. Yet while they'd been correctly deemed alpha billionaires, powerful men who controlled their worlds, their fans and followers missed one important facet: Their shared goal to better their world.

Royce lifted his glass. "No one discovered your true identity."

"At least not for a while." Dominick sipped from his own goblet. The thousand dollar a bottle brew tingled on his tongue. "You know how the story ends."

"I'd say the story ended quite well," Aidan Bancroft rubbed his hands together. "I must say, I am quite jealous of your fortune. You have a beautiful wife."

The others nodded their agreement. It was quite a compliment, from men the whole world envied. Yet it was not the attainment of a relationship, for each of them were chased, but of the beautiful union he now shared.

With Adrianna, life was perfect.

His days were filled with delightful conversations and invigorating adventures, his nights, holding the woman he loved. Being with her was a journey, filled with more beauty than he could ever imagine. The present was a gift, the future destiny's path. He couldn't wait to see what it wrought.

His business had seen as much success, after they rid it of the corruption lurking within. Carlyle was now in prison, along with Dobbs and the other criminals who infiltrated it for personal gain. Knight Technology was once again one of the best companies to work for, along with Adrianna's new venture, which was taking the computer world by storm. Together they were going to change the world – just like they had changed each other.

And although these men had almost all one could desire – wealth, power, fame – only he and Royce had found love. With their popularity, it wasn't the lack of opportunity, yet a wariness that comes after being chased for so long. When these men found the right women, they would be the hunters.

"Cameron is also happy for you, not that he would ever admit it."

Dominick nodded at the mention of the one member of their group not present. The billionaire lawyer portrayed nothing but power and control. "Wasn't he supposed to attend tonight?"

Aidan frowned. "He texted me after his business meeting. He was skipping the early flight for a later drive, only they're having massive storms right now."

Dominick put down his glass. "He's driving in dangerous conditions?" He grasped his cell phone and typed a message. He placed down the phone, yet his concern intensified, even as the conversation resumed. When the phone rang, he answered it on the first ring. "Knight here."

"It's me." Cameron's voice was low and hushed. Behind it, a thundering roar sounded. No, *literal* thunder.

"Is everything all right, Cameron? It sounds like a hurricane out there."

"I'm fine." Yet the words were a whisper, the tone urgent. Something was definitely happening.

"You don't sound fine," Dominick said bluntly.

"Alexander, are you all right?" Now a third voice spoke, a *female* one. "Did you take off your clothing?"

All concern fled. "Well, that explains it."

"It's not what you think." The whisper was even lower this time. "I'm not here for an affair. I don't even know her."

"That would be worse."

A low chuckle broke the sobriety. "I'm serious. You see, she's under the impression I'm an actor she's hired."

"Excuse me?" The other men in the room stared at Dominick's exclamation, their varying expressions of curiosity and amusement demanding an explanation. He waved them off. "How would she get that impression?"

"I can't explain now." Rustling sounded in the background. "I may be gone for a while." Another pause, a lower whisper. "I better go. I have a part to play."

Cameron had never acted in his life. Was he pursuing a greater role than even he imagined? Dominick clicked off the phone, as the men looked at him expectantly.

"What was that?" Aidan leaned forward. "That sounded… unusual."

"I'm not sure." Dominick slowly shook his head. "But it's going to be quite a story."

UNDERCOVER BILLIONAIRE

Thank you for reading Billionaire in Disguise. I hope you enjoyed my characters and world. My next book, Undercover Billionaire, is available now in Kindle Unlimited.

Chapter 1

"And, that, ladies and gentlemen, is why I shall be victorious."

From any other man, the statement would have been boastful, exaggerated or most likely both, a product of overconfidence, arrogance and a distinct dearth of modesty. Yet his confidence was warranted, the arrogance, though present, was tolerated, and no complaint given for the lack of modesty.

For it was simply true.

Cameron Drake was a man who achieved his goals. He wielded power like a warrior, wrapped in a tycoon's golden thread, his hair a rich auburn, his emerald eyes shimmering with fierce intelligence. His face was chiseled perfection, curves and angles masterfully formed, with full sensual lips and high cheekbones. He rose inches over six feet, with a heavily muscled body no Armani suit could disguise.

Yet far more than physical features made this man the center of attention, as he gazed at a courtroom filled with million-dollar lawyers, powerful politicians and a corporate defendant who saw no reason not to dump toxic waste in a freshwater lake. The defendant was spending millions to keep doing it.

Cameron was not going to let that happen.

He represented a group of people, who joined together to fight the international juggernaut that would destroy pristine lakes, home and hearth to an aquatic wonderland. They couldn't afford a law firm like the one he owned, in which millions exchanged hands, yet for this case, it didn't matter. He had billions, which meant he could defend the causes he believed in – pro bono.

Cameron stood still, seconds after the closing arguments, commanding the courtroom like Poseidon ruled the sea. The jury watched silently, portraits of emotion from his riveting speech, as his clients beamed in delighted disbelief, their confidence evidenced by watery eyes. And the defendants? Their horrified expressions revealed their destruction was over.

Indeed, this man always got what he wanted.

Yet despite collecting legal wins like a child gathers trading cards, Cameron had been restless recently. Something seemed missing – something or someone. For most people, this restlessness would have elicited a tangle of hopelessness, frustration or despair, yet challenges only invigorated him. It focused him on the hunt, propelled him to victory. Whatever would cure the restlessness, he would find it.

"Moist chocolate fudge brownie covered in raspberry ganache."

A soft sigh, a turning page.

"Strawberry shortcake with freshly whipped cream."

Another page, and this time a gasp.

"Whoa. Rocky Road, Dulce de Leche and Chocolate Chip Cookie Dough ice cream, smothered in hot fudge, dripping in gooey caramel and covered with glitter sprinkles and three cherries. Strike that, the entire bottle of cherries."

Kaitlyn Owens tiptoed through the room, edging towards the woman whose nose actually touched the tablet. The photograph showed an iconic surfer with golden blond hair and simpering blue eyes, gazing into the camera with come-hither adoration. Kaitlyn stopped directly behind the woman. "I'd say Special Value Instant Oatmeal, the banana – no, the prune – type."

Kaitlyn grinned as Allison, her closest and oldest friend, jumped and pivoted, flushing at being caught indulging in one succulent sundae. Standing in the backroom of The Candy Cane Bakery and Confectionary, the woman was supposed to be helping in the honest work of chocolate and pastry production, but instead of toiling in the trenches of flour and sugar, she had been distracted by hot buns of a different type.

Yet the guilt quickly transformed into disbelief. "Are you nuts? Just look at him, at all of them! They're perfect..."

Had she missed something? Kaitlyn commandeered the tablet, flipping through the pages of so-called delicacies. They were a cornucopia of romance novel heroes, from blond movie stars to tall, dark and handsome princes – chiseled, defined and heavily muscled. Her answer was obvious. "Yup, definitely prune instant oatmeal."

Her friend sighed, as if she knew further argument would be fruitless and simply hadn't the strength to try. "All right," she conceded, abandoning her precious gossip website and striding to the worktable. "So my dream man and his friends are instant oatmeal." At Kaitlyn's pointed look, she elaborated, "The prune type. Then who could possibly rank ice cream sundae in the opinion of picky Miss Owens?"

Kaitlyn joined her friend on the bench and gazed at the small chamber filled to the brim with candy-making equipment and supplies. Rainbow walls and glittering floors accentuated silver racks, laden with whimsical cakes and pastries. The air was fresh and sweet, scented with fresh chocolate chip cookies and vanilla cake. This was her dream come true, a sweet Florida candy and pastry store built with hard work and dedication. After years of toiling, the small shop finally turned a profit, and business was booming. Best of all, she earned enough to give back to the community through free workshops and donations to those in need.

"First let me say I do not need or desire a man, but if I did…" A vision formed, the easy-going man who would fit perfectly into her hectic life. "He would be average sized, probably not very big or muscular. He doesn't have to be the greatest looking of men, but nice and modest. Quiet and shy, yet considerate and good. He would listen to me. He would be very agreeable and sort of… what's the word? Mellow. Yes, mellow."

"That's your perfect 10?" Allison gaped. "Are you certain you're not talking about a puppy?"

Kaitlyn laughed. She attracted her fair share of men, yet the type of male who pursued her left much to be desired. Her last three boyfriends, Mr. Wrong, Mr. Really Wrong and Mr. I-Thought-Neanderthals-Were-Extinct Wrong, proved

MELANIE KNIGHT

that. Big and burly, aggressive and narcissistic, the men were more interested in a trophy girlfriend than in a true woman or relationship. If she ever had time to date, she would choose a non-aggressive gentleman who would let her be who and what she wanted. "Sounds perfect to me." Kaitlyn grabbed a handful of gooey cookie dough and began to shape miniature hearts. "But it doesn't matter anyway. Like I said, I don't need a man."

"Mail call!"

Kaitlyn smiled as the letter carrier, an elderly man with soft laugh lines etched on his kindly face, placed a thick pile on the side bench. "Good morning, Frank. How are you?"

"Wonderful." Aged eyes sparkled with mirth. "Thank you again for the surprise gift basket for the wife. It cheered her right up after the surgery."

"Of course." She smiled warmly. "On your way out, stop by the counter. I have a little something for both of you."

His ruddy cheeks deepened. "You don't have to spoil us."

Perhaps not, but it felt great.

She palmed another handful of sticky batter, halted as an unobtrusive letter peeked out from under the stack. She placed down the batter, wiped her hands on her apron and reached for the small brown envelope.

Her heart stuttered as she uncovered the return address. She clutched the envelope tighter, crinkling it in pale fingers, before swiftly tearing it open, accidently ripping the folded note within. The scent of cheap perfume tickled her nose as she brought out a thin piece of paper with three single sentences:

I'm taking you up on your standing offer. See you Friday for a week visit. I can't wait to meet your better half. Cynthia

She read the contents of the missive. Then she read it again. She read it once more. And yet its contents remained

104

the same, the modern version of a gauntlet thrown from across the country.

"What is it?" Allison asked in a low voice. All signs of mirth had vanished, in a charged atmosphere that couldn't be missed. "Has something happened?"

Kaitlyn folded the offending letter and placed it into the envelope. She picked up the batter for the next heart, moving in methodical motions, as the letter repeated itself in her mind. She made a dozen hearts before her hands stilled on the mushy batter. She let out a deep, low breath. "I never thought it would come to this," she whispered.

Allison brought her hands to her lips, her expression tinted with dread. "What is it?"

Then Kaitlyn uttered the most tragic words ever voiced in human existence:

"I need a man."

Allison stood silent, too shocked to speak. Kaitlyn breathed deeply. Her friend clearly appreciated the grave implications of the statement. Caught in a position of vulnerability and the need for... a man. The situation deserved a moment of silence.

"I'm sorry." Allison shook her head. "I thought you said..."

"I need a man," Kaitlyn repeated miserably. "I don't believe it."

"Neither do I. But backtrack for a second." Alison pointed to the folded paper. "I'm assuming your announcement has to do with that letter."

"Unfortunately." Kaitlyn picked up the discarded piece of mail, keeping it at arm's length as if a rabid dog poised to bite. "My cousin Cynthia has decided to visit. In just a few days she will invade my home, where she will expect my boyfriend and I to welcome her."

"Boyfriend?" Allison opened her mouth, closed it. "You have a boyfriend?"

MELANIE KNIGHT

"No. Yes. No." Kaitlyn rubbed the bridge of her nose, where a dull ache had started to throb. Her cousin hadn't yet arrived and already she was upending her life. "As children, Cynthia deemed it her mission to best me in any and every way possible. It is a practice she's carried into adulthood."

"Sounds like she never made it past her teens."

"Precisely. Every so often she calls to gloat about this or that, always in a sugar-coated manner that rubs me like fingernails on a chalkboard. A couple of years ago, she spent an hour bragging about her wonderful boyfriend and ridiculing my lack thereof. I finally had enough. I concocted a story about a fictional boyfriend and enjoyed a splendid afternoon convincing her I scored the greatest man of the season."

She shrugged. "I never thought it would matter. How could she ever discover my lie? She's not on social media and doesn't keep in touch with the rest of the family, at least not since the incident at my cousin's wedding, which involved several groomsmen, an extraordinary amount of tequila and not a lot of clothing." She winced. "According to this letter, however, she's coming in three days and is very excited to see my fairytale prince. Which is why I have to start kissing every frog in town."

"But it still doesn't make sense." Allison held up her hands. "You go after what you want, and I've never seen you afraid of anyone. Why don't you just tell her the truth?"

"I can't." Kaitlyn breathed out. "I'm not embarrassed or ashamed I don't have a fairytale prince, if he even exists. Like I said before, I don't want or need him, and I'll tell that to a thousand Cynthias. I just don't want her to know I got worked up enough to lie about it. Could you imagine her gloating to every relative from my mother to fifth cousin? She'd end the family feud just to do it!"

Allison frowned. "Couldn't you just tell her you broke up?"

If only it were that easy. "It won't work. Cynthia may be horrible, but she's not stupid. Whenever she asked about him, I said things were going great. I kept meaning to tell her we broke up but then she'd gloat, and it was just easier to maintain the ruse. Unfortunately, she called last week for her annual 'I'm better than you' conversation, and I mentioned him. If I don't produce Mr. Wonderful, she'll assume I lied. Same thing if I tell her she can't come."

Allison looked at the letter. "Why would she even want to come? It doesn't sound like you're best buddies."

"We're not. The standing invitation was given ten years ago! After mentioning some issues with a current boyfriend and a former best friend – three guesses on what happened there – she asked if I was going to be in town for the next few weeks. She knows I have nothing big planned. Things must have gotten complicated, and since she's insulted every other relative, she's using me as free rent until the situation calms." She raked her hand through her hair. "If I can just get through this visit, I promise to invent a quick breakup and never lie again. Yet where am I going to find a prince in just three days?"

A mischievous grin lit Allison's face. "Oh, you don't need actual royalty. You just need someone to play him. And I know exactly where to look."

When Allison first suggested finding a man through a brochure, Kaitlyn assumed she'd been joking. Pick a man out of a catalog? It sounded like something from a torrid 90's movie. However, after a thorough explanation, the idea sounded not only feasible but logical. She didn't need a man, she needed one to pretend to be her man. Who could do the job better than an actor?

And where could she find an actor on such short notice? To her astonishment, they actually made brochures for that type of thing, and her friend had them. Apparently, Allison, a private investigator, used some of the companies on prior cases, all of which turned out successful. She'd gladly lent Kaitlyn the pamphlets.

Now she sat on the plush jacquard sofa of her brightly lit living room, clutching one of the brochures. Kaitlyn lived on the floor above her store, in a small apartment converted from an unfinished loft. Scented with the delicious aromas of cookies and cakes, it had only a single bedroom and bathroom, but an open floor plan combined with aesthetically placed decorations created an atmosphere that seemed almost spacious. Pine furniture, flowering plants and posters of scenic landscapes created a charming space, perfect for destressing after a long day of candy creating.

Now she was searching for a delicacy of a different type. An actor would be perfect for her situation. She wouldn't have to worry about the calamities of a normal relationship – fighting, break-ups, messy emotions. No risk of an explosive fight or lover's quarrel in front of the ever-watchful Cynthia. And best of all, she could specify exactly the type of man she wanted. No aggressive, self-righteous, full-of-himself man for her. It was the ultimate solution.

Kaitlyn held up the most promising brochure: The Actors Association. The rates seemed reasonable, the operation professional. They hailed from Houston, far from the Florida town of Greenfield she called home, but they boasted nationwide coverage. Since they flew someone out, it cost a decent amount – payable upfront – but the success of the shop afforded her a little extra cash. She dialed the number and was immediately connected with a receptionist who confirmed availability and price.

Everything appeared legitimate, and yet still she hesitated. Could she really hire an actor to pretend to be her boyfriend? A picture of Cynthia flashed, and she notched up her chin. "I'm ready to place my order."

In a daze, Kaitlyn answered the receptionist's questions, paid by credit card and reluctantly scheduled the actor for the very next day. Cynthia would arrive Friday night, and it was already Tuesday. Unfortunately, the time to prepare with the actor had to take priority over the time to prepare for the actor. She refused to compromise on one aspect, however – the type of man she'd be shackled to for Cynthia's visit.

When the clerk asked for performer specifications, Kaitlyn launched into her speech. "Not too big or aggressive. Mild-mannered, calm and quiet. Maybe not exactly meek, but well, actually meek sounds great. Easy-going with a capital E. Someone who will listen to me and do what is expected without a problem."

She might have to share a fictitious relationship, but it would be with a man she could tolerate. The receptionist assured her they had the perfect performer, who fit her description exactly. He would arrive at 8 o'clock sharp the next evening.

Ignoring the slight feeling of uneasiness that accompanies one's hiring of a stranger to play a loving boyfriend, Kaitlyn agreed to the terms and completed the call.

Tomorrow loomed like a threatening storm. For the first time in years, a man would hover, pretending to be her boyfriend. Would he look at her with come-hither eyes, pepper feather-light touches on her body? Not only must she allow it, but she would encourage it. As she got ready for bed, she couldn't quite quell her worries, strangely more intense over the actor's arrival than that of her cousin. All would be well...

As long as she kept control.

Wednesday morning dawned in stormy glory. Gray clouds darkened a sunless sky, all traces of cerulean hidden beneath their gloomy depths. Howling winds blew through rickety old trees and over weathered grasses, sending wet leaves scattering through the air. Kaitlyn slept through her alarm, and only the rumbling of thunder finally roused her from slumber.

In minutes, she consumed a morning meal of cereal and toast, then spent half an hour selecting an outfit. She donned a silk cream-colored blouse with a wide scoop neckline and sheer sleeves, which mixed femininity and businesswoman to harmonious perfection. The matching silk skirt fell to just above her knees, ending in a wisp of sheer chiffon. Long enough to be casual, but short enough to show off her legs, the skirt seemingly floated around her. A single diamond solitaire on an elegant golden chain completed the outfit.

She raced down to the store and completed her morning preparations. In addition to all sorts of candy, the store offered a variety of cakes and pastries, baked from the freshest ingredients each day. She passed a fudge supreme cake dripping in chocolate, a strawberry shortcake with homemade whipped cream and chocolate croissants still warm from the oven. Her employees had already started crafting the morning's delicacies, scenting the air with their delicious aroma.

Kaitlyn gave a warm greeting to Lily, her baker, and started setting out the rest of the morning displays. Time passed quickly, and the opening hour soon rolled around. Despite the turbulent weather, the store grew busy, and time whizzed by in a hectic but enjoyable rush. It was not until late afternoon that she finally noticed how bad the storm had become. The once light gray sky loomed as dark as night, setting a horror movie backdrop to the thick raindrops that pelted against the windows, hard enough to shake the sturdy glass. Large balls of hail accompanied the rain, shattering against the sidewalk in deafening crashes like a marching band's drum, only to be drowned out by the incessant rumbling of thunder. Now concerned about her actor's imminent arrival, Kaitlyn left the store in her employees' capable hands and hurried upstairs to call the acting company.

The same receptionist answered the phone and listened as Kaitlyn apprised her of the situation. The clerk knew of the inclement weather and assured her the flight should arrive on time despite the storm. If the actor couldn't make it that night, he would be there early the next morning.

The afternoon passed almost as quickly as the morning, although business was slower for the nastiness outside. At half past seven, Kaitlyn finished the last of her closing procedures and returned to her apartment. Since the actor would provide his own transportation from the airport, she hadn't recorded his airline information. With no way to check if his flight arrived as scheduled, she could do nothing but wait.

Another bolt of thunder raged, and the lights flickered, amidst a disturbing thought. Originally, she planned to house the actor in a hotel a few blocks away, even during her cousin's visit. She would pretend he wanted to give her quality time alone with her cousin, which would reduce the risk of Cynthia uncovering the ruse. If he managed to arrive safely, however, she couldn't possibly send him out again in Greenfield's own virtual hurricane.

Like it or not, she would be sharing the house with a stranger, at least for the night.

She caught sight of the brochure, smiled and relaxed. There was nothing to fear. Her specified man would be no more threatening than a kitten, and probably just as small. Satisfied with logic's reassurance, she curled up on the cozy couch, a romance novel in one hand and a glass of white zinfandel in the other, to await the beckoning of the doorbell.

Eight o'clock arrived with neither the actor's arrival nor a phone call. No problem. She wasn't really, really, really, really grateful for the delay or anything. Even if the plane arrived on time, the performer would likely move slower in the midst of the storm. She waited and waited, putting down the book when she re-read the same scene four times. Nine o'clock arrived, followed swiftly by ten. Fate had granted a reprieve; likely her guest would not arrive until the next day. She all but did a happy dance. Okay, she actually did perform a happy dance, but it was a small one. Relieved for reasons she wouldn't explore, she reclined on the soft sofa and allowed sleep to overtake her.

"Damn!"

The late model Porsche hydroplaned through the dangerously wet roads, squealing in indignation as the lone driver jerked the steering wheel to the left. A tree appeared out of the darkness, solid and thick and closer and closer and... he veered to the right, swiping as close to the jagged bark as a lover's caress.

Narrowly missing another fallen tree, Cameron Drake regained control of the embattled vehicle, exhaling air heavy with the scent of rain and oak, even in the luxurious cabin. Lightning flashed and thunder boomed, heralding his close call, the third almost-catastrophe in as many minutes. Would he emerge intact from the next one?

He drove with restraint, moving as slowly as possible, yet the vicious storm pounded and pummeled the world around him, unforgivable and unrelenting. Like it or not, the elements held Cameron at their mercy tonight. Frustrating and exasperating for a man accustomed to ruling his world.

No sane person would be on the road on such a night, as a virtual hurricane loomed from above. He hadn't even planned to come through the small town, but half the roads on his typical route were impassible, the other half dangerous. How had something so right turned so very wrong?

It had been a good day, a great one even. He won yet another case, awarding the firm that bore his name another win against those who would destroy the environment. He argued the trial in Gainesville, which, difficult as it was to believe, resided relatively close to his current location. After the case, his colleagues took the first flight back to Miami, and although he held a golden ticket with the same destination, he foolishly declined. More work remained to wrap up the logistics of the case. Leave a job unfinished? That was not how he became the overnight star of the legal world.

At thirty-three years of age, Cameron already posed a major player. He'd worked his way up from a modest upbringing to receive a full scholarship to Harvard. From there he progressed to law school, graduating at the top of his class. He had been accepted into a prestigious law firm in Miami, became their prodigy and won case after case. In an unheard-of scarcity of years, Cameron had branched off into his own multibillion-dollar firm. Now the owner and senior partner of The Drake Association, he'd finally achieved his goals, and was part of the elite group the press dubbed the Billionaires of Miami.

He'd traded his plane ticket for an evening flight, which gave him plenty of time to finish his work. Unfortunately, the elements didn't respect his dedication as much as the legal field and upended his flight. Instead of taking a one-day hiatus from the Association, he decided to drive. How hard could it be? Yet as he swerved around another fallen branch, the answer was clear:

Too hard.

He let out another slow breath, squinting past the rapidly swaying yet hopelessly outmaneuvered windshield wipers. Three droplets replaced every one it felled, leaving a small river flowing above his dash. A thundering gale shook the vehicle, its tendrils reaching a towering oak mere yards ahead. He hit the brakes, skidding as the tree swayed back and forth, one way and then another like a drunk ballroom dancer. The tree shook and crunched, crackled and then....

Snapped.

The world seemingly moved in slow motion, as the massive tree fell, down, down, down. The car was slowing, but was it enough? With a thunderous boom, the tree crashed into the ground.... just missing him.

Cameron eased his foot back onto the accelerator. He had to find shelter, and he had to find it now. Even a stranger's house couldn't be more dangerous than nature's fury. Of course, his third degree black belt could help just in case he picked the one mass murderer on the road. As if by fate's mercy, a light sparkled in the distance. The car slowly rumbled its way to the sanctuary.

The Candy Cane Bakery and Confectionary. A frivolous moniker, but somehow fitting for the town of Green-whatever-the-second-part-of-the-name-is. Cloaked in darkness, the store sat deserted, but a light shone from a window up above. A spiral staircase led to an apartment over the shop.

Cameron didn't hesitate before turning into the narrow driveway. He had no choice, not unless he preferred to camp in a ditch. He maneuvered the car through a shallow river of mud to what was hopefully a parking space next to an older Toyota. His tires sputtered and protested, seemingly breathing a deep sigh of relief when he turned off the ignition. Of course, he didn't have an umbrella, so on the count of three, he used all his strength to push the door open against the howling wind.

Outside the world thundered like a runaway train, a sea of darkness illuminated by flashes of brilliant electricity. Icy rain pelted his skin, burning his eyes and soaking his clothing. Cameron sprinted through the torrential rain to the staircase, as wind, leaves and branches swirled around him. His $1,500 A. Testoni shoes sank into the mud, and water pelted a Rolex that cost ten times more. He clutched the slippery side rail as he hiked up the stairs two at a time, making it to the front door in thirty seconds flat.

He had no idea of what to expect from the owner of a store called The Candy Cane, as he rang the doorbell. It might take some of his best lawyer skills to convince him – or her – to let him in. That was okay – he was used to convincing people to do what he wanted.

After all, he was always in control.

EAR-SPLITTING RINGING SHOOK THE WORLD, jerking Kaitlyn to consciousness. She shot up, tangled in a sea of blankets, as the terrible intrusion splintered the air once more. Outside, the storm raged, the rain beating a rapid drum, set to the heavy bass of thunder. She scanned the space, yet all was calm and peaceful in the small living room, the air cool, the book still opened to where she'd stopped the night below. As the fogginess lifted, her heart slowed. The "terrible ringing" was nothing more than the doorbell, a jolting yet innocuous interruption to slumber.

Then she froze, relief vanishing like the morning fog.

Who would visit at such an hour, through a raging tempest? It could only be one person:

The actor.

She hastily tumbled out of her makeshift bed, nearly falling to the floor in her rush. She still wore her work clothes, but they could no longer claim professional savvy after being slept in on a less-than-spacious sofa. Smoothing herself out as best she could, she strode to the door. How had the actor made it? How had he driven through the horrible weather? How had the plane even landed?

The details didn't matter now. Kaitlyn unlocked the first bolt, but then hesitated. Although his identity was obvious, a single woman living alone must be cautious. "Who's there?"

The man responded just as booming thunder rocked the wooden building to its frame. Beneath the incessant rumbling, she caught only part of a name – Drake, maybe – and the word "Association." But that was enough. Who else from the Actors Association would call on the eve of a virtual typhoon? She fortified herself, unlocked the door and flung it open.

Whether or not she erred in opening the door, she most certainly miscalculated in opening it wide. A fierce wind instantly grabbed hold of it, slamming the light wood panel against the building with a splintering bang. Kaitlyn grabbed for the knob, yet it slipped in her hand as the tempest bested her in a game of tug-o-war. The rain stung her like a thousand bees, soaking her instantly. Water swept into the apartment, carried on the arms of a strong, unrelenting gale.

The man stood like a ghostly apparition, a shadowy warrior illuminated by electrifying bolts of lightning. Taut limbs froze, and she could do nothing but stare at the two fearsome displays of nature – the raging storm and the man whose power rivalled it. Then with almost superhuman speed, he burst into the apartment, moving into her once private safe haven. He grabbed the door and slammed it shut, as if the wind were no more than a gentle breeze. For the first time, he was clearly visible.

Oh. My. Goodness.

This had to be a mistake. A very big, very muscular, very powerful mistake. This man – no, this giant – could absolutely, positively, 150 billion percent not be her new boyfriend. Power radiated from well-built muscles, unrelenting strength focused like a laser beam on her. Oh-please-donotletthisbehim-no.

Domineering and powerful, he towered above her. Not merely tall, he boasted the body of a Medieval warrior, defined by a broad chest, strong arms and a domineering stance. His face held as strong definition as his body, with a chiseled jawline and striking features that brought to life the most handsome male she had ever seen. With deep auburn hair and eyes as green as a cat, he possessed a fierce presence few could match.

This man fit her description perfectly?! Anything but small, he would most certainly never accept the word weak as a description, neither physically nor mentally. And with no time to hire another actor, she had no choice but to pretend to love this man, this warrior who would stay with her in the apartment tonight... alone. Taking a deep breath, she gave the only appropriate response:

"Oh crap."

UNDERCOVER BILLIONAIRE IS AVAILABLE NOW, free in Kindle Unlimited.

WOULD YOU LIKE A FREE NOVELLA?

Sign up for my newsletter at www.

MelanieKnightAuthor.com and receive The Billionaire's Secret Wife.

The Billionaire's Secret Wife

SHE MARRIED a man she'd never met. Why won't he let her go?

Marry a man she'd never met? Outrageous, ridiculous, *impossible*. Yet to save her nephew, Elora Livingston weds powerful billionaire Royce Livingston, separated by continents in a virtual wedding. The marriage was supposed to be temporary, even as they grow ever-closer through letters and phone calls. She must leave the fantasy, but…

He won't let her go.

Donning a disguise, she infiltrates a glittering charity ball at his lavish mansion, determined to dissolve the marriage once and for all. Yet unexpected desires soar, forging a connection she cannot deny. No one knows the woman in their midst is the powerful man's wife, as one question burns above all:

Does he recognize her?

His wife thinks he married her to gain an inheritance, but Royce Livingston has altogether different motives. He cannot ignore the connection with the alluring woman, built through a thousand stories and endless conversations. As secrets swirl, he fights for the most important merger in his life. He will show her what life is like as…

The Billionaire's Secret Wife.

Books in The Secret Billionaire's Series:

Billionaire in Disguise

When Adriana recruits her company's newest intern to pretend to be her boyfriend, she has no idea he's actually the billionaire CEO in disguise.

Undercover Billionaire

Kaitlyn hires an actor to be her fake boyfriend, only the powerful man isn't what she ordered. It's a case of mistaken identity, but the billionaire lawyer goes along with the ruse.

The Billionaire's Secret Baby

What if you had to tell a man he was a father - not of an unborn life, not of a swaddled infant, but of a child of four? Sound difficult? Then how about this: What if you had to tell a man you never met?

For exclusive news, giveaways and surprises, subscribe to my newsletter at www.MelanieKnightAuthor.com.

I love connecting with readers on social media. **The Secret Crusaders: Melanie's Romance Readers is my Facebook group for everything romance.**

Follow me on Social Media:

Facebook
Tiktok

MELANIE KNIGHT

I also write historical Regency romance under the name Melanie Rose Clarke. Check out my books, all available now in Kindle Unlimited.
Escaping the Duke
Captured by the Earl
The Untamed Duke

THE SECRET BILLIONAIRES SERIES

Billionaire in Disguise

Wanted: Fake boyfriend

Qualifications: Must be charming and friendly. No criminal masterminds. Prior experience as a fake boyfriend a plus.

Responsibilities: Convince my large family you are my boyfriend, so I don't ruin their celebration. May involve shirtless jogs, splash fights and lots of practice kissing.

Applicant Name: Dominick Knight, a.k.a. Nick Walters

Employment: Billionaire CEO of Knight Technology, undercover as a temp to investigate corruption.

Special skills: Keeping my true identity a secret.

✯

Final result: Secrets, seduction and excitement.

Undercover Billionaire

Her: She's sassy, intelligent and strong, and she's had enough of men trying to run her life. Problem is, she needs a man – and quick – to be the non-existent fiancé she's been bragging about to the family. Enter Drake Alexander, hired with the best of credentials from a top-notch acting association. Only he's not exactly what she's ordered...

Him: He's rich, powerful and just a little bit arrogant, and he doesn't need any more women running after his billions. Problem is, he's stuck in the storm of the century in some hole-in-the-wall town. Banging on the door of a local, the last thing he expects is to be greeted by a beautiful woman ranting about how he's the preposterously late actor she's been expecting. Yet for some reason, he lets her believe the lie....

Kaitlyn has no choice but to accept Drake as her pretend fiancé, even though he invades her thoughts and unsettles her life. Worse yet, continues to play his role even when her family is not around! Soon they're planning a pretend wedding, getting closer and closer to "I do." Sparks fire and suspicions soar, but everything changes when...

The truth is revealed.

The Billionaire's Secret Child

What if you had to tell a man he was a father - not of an unborn life, not of a swaddled infant, but of a child of four?

Sound difficult? Then how about this:

What if you had to tell a man you never met?

Reporter Laura Blake always imagined she would have a child the old-fashioned way, but when life didn't work out that way, she conceived her daughter through the wonders of technology. Five years later, life is perfect... until her father's two heart attacks, and a newfound quest emerges: find the man who fathered her child to attain potentially life-saving medical records. Only the anonymous donor is not the stranger she imagined, but Aidan Bancroft, famous billionaire known for attaining what and who he wants. Furthermore…

He never was an anonymous donor.

Aidan is furious when a reporter confronts him with impossible claims. He only visited the fertility clinic to conceive with his late wife, and lost everything. Yet soon it becomes clear there is far more to her story. He will discover everything there is to know about Laura Blake and her child.

Stunned by the news and their life-altering ramifications, Laura flees, hoping for time to carve the future. Yet Aidan follows her, his suspicions forging his own investigation. As passions soar and emotions flourish, they delve closer and closer. Soon Aidan is chasing more than his suspicions.

What happens when the truth is revealed?

ABOUT THE AUTHOR

Melanie Rose Clarke has wanted to be a writer since she was a little girl. Sixteen years ago, she married her own hero, and now she creates compelling stories with strong heroines, powerful males and, of course, happily every afters. She writes historical (regency) romance, contemporary romance, paranormal romance, romantic suspense and women's fiction.

Melanie is a three-time Golden Heart® finalist. Her manuscripts have earned numerous awards in writing competitions, including several first place showings. With over two decades of professional writing experience, Melanie has written thousands of pieces for businesses and individual clients. She has worked in advertising and marketing, and her freelance articles on the web have garnered hundreds of thousands of views.

She writes amidst her five beautiful children, her dream come true. Besides writing, she loves to read, exercise and spend time outdoors. She is a member of Mensa. For more information, visit her website at www.MelanieKnightAuthor.com.

Made in the USA
Columbia, SC
05 October 2024